Praise for The Songbird's Sting

"An exciting, fast-moving chase adventure peopled with women and men tougher than saddle leather. Fans of Louis L'Amour will appreciate plenty of action peppered with historic details." –Debbie Burke, Award-Winning Journalist and Author.

"Larry Martin, a seasoned writer of over 60 novels, has the formula down for writing another fast paced, action packed western novel. I guarantee you'll be turning the pages fast to see how the story ends." –Sue Ready, *Ever Ready Book Reviews*

"I really enjoyed this book. The action grabbed you from page 1 and kept your attention clear to the end. Any fan of Louis L'Amour should like this book." –Kelly Creek, advanced reader

THE SONGBIRD'S STING

******

The Arizona Series

L.J. MARTIN

WOLFPACK
PUBLISHING
— EST 2013 —

Paperback Edition
Copyright © 2021 L.J. Martin

Wolfpack Publishing
5130 S. Fort Apache Road 215-380
Las Vegas, NV 89148

wolfpackpublishing.com

Paperback ISBN 978-1-64734-280-7
eBook ISBN 978-1-64734-279-1

THE SONGBIRD'S STING

******

Chapter One

***

With an unladylike gesture, she stepped daintily out of the Arizona Territorial Express Company office, stretched and yawned. She had a long trip ahead. Suddenly she collapsed to a knee and screamed as the post beside her splintered, and the roar of a gunshot echoed up and down Whiskey Row.

She glanced right just in time to see two men stumbling out of the Palace Saloon and Hotel, locked in a struggle half a block away. Two more shots rang out, one from each revolver in the hand of the two men, each wrist locked in the free hand of the other. Then a knee came up, and the man who took it in the crotch folded and collapsed. The man remaining on his feet clubbed the other, and he went to his back. With deliberation, the standing man cocked his revolver and fired almost point-blank into the other's forehead. Even from that distance, she could see the downed man's hair afire and saw the splatter of bone, gray matter, and blood.

She turned away with revulsion, realizing that the many men on the boardwalk had scattered—some back into the office, some behind the Concord Coach, which sat awaiting its passengers.

She returned her gaze to the macabre scene. The shooter didn't hesitate but ran to his handsome chestnut mount at the hitching rail, jerked the loosely tied reins, mounted, and gave spurs to the tall horse.

As he galloped by, he locked eyes with Elizabeth for a moment. They were strikingly blue under a shock of black hair that protruded from under a fawn-colored hat. And to her surprise, he touched his hat brim politely and laughed. Then all she saw through her equally blue eyes was his back disappearing and dust billowing and clods flying behind.

Men started filtering out of the Express Company office and back onto the boardwalk, and went back to the business at hand. A strongbox, obviously heavy, was carried from the office and loaded into the boot, and it was quickly hidden by baggage. She was surprised to note Wells Fargo Co. printed on the box, although this was not that line.

She shook her head as an older disheveled man displaced himself from hiding behind the coach and approached, a cigar clamped in his teeth.

"A wee bit of excitement, eh, little lady?" he asked, hissing a little through missing and blackened teeth.

"Yes. God's will and mere inches it's not me bound for the digger. He must have plans for me." She glanced heavenward then back up the block at the fallen man. Others had now gathered around him, some with hands on knees, staring down as if a meteorite had landed and required their inspection.

One of the onlookers poured his beer on the downed man's face, she presumed to extinguish his smoldering hair. There would be no waking him.

Elizabeth shook her head in consternation, then glanced

at the man loading and securing her bags into the coach boot. She was so very happy to be leaving Prescott. But not nearly so happy as she'd been the night before last to see her brother riding away with his kin, escaping a lynching, a sympathy that had stirred through the city's saloons with a vindictive roar.

The grizzled old man, now totally ignoring the happenings up the street, as if the occurrence was as common as a crow perched on the eaves above, approached and eyed her up and down through watery, faded gray eyes as if she was a prime rib of beef, cooked to a turn and ready to bite.

Never one to shirk, she eyed him back, but with more of a glare than with admiration. "Are you handling the reins of this stage, sir?"

"I am the whip, ma'am. Oliver Tidwell at your service. Best man on the ribbons this side of the Mississippi, and don't mind saying so. And y'all are fortunate to be in my care. I presume you're my passenger?"

She answered only with a slight disgusted nod, so he continued. "'Course I never been on the far side of the big river."

"In your care? Not by choice, sir, for it seems I have little choice in the matter. When the devil is Prescott going to get a rail service?"

"Dang sure hope never, or I'll be looking for other employment."

"Is it always this bloody hot in May?" she asked. "Not to speak of violent."

"Y'all think this is hot? Sounds like you'd be a John Bull? Don't she never get hot in England?"

Ignoring his question, she turned to watch the conductor who would ride to the left of the whip, or driver, and serve as a shotgun guard. He continued to load and secure her trunk and four matching English mahogany-colored cases, one a round hatbox. She was surprised at how easily the very short man handled them. He was no taller than she, only 5'2" or so, but two and a half times her weight, and light on his feet for an obese man. The bags gleamed, nicely trimmed with brass fittings, and she did not want them scarred nor scratched. Satisfied, she returned her gaze to the whip, who was enthusiastically chomping his cigar. "My cases are loaded. Your hand, please."

"All them fancy satchels your'n?" he asked, a bemused smirk changed the arrangement of his wrinkles under the gray stubble. "That there is a handful for Tubby."

"Tubby?" She asked.

"You sure as the devil wouldn't call the fat boy 'bean pole', now would ya?"

She ignored the question. "They are mine, and your division agent was not bashful about charging me two dollars extra. I hope your conductor has secured them properly."

"Tubby ties 'em tight as a tick in a lamb's tail," he said. Amused, the whip offered his hand and with the other on her elbow, helped her mount the step and slip into the coach. As she was first to load, it felt roomy to her small five-foot-two-inch frame. Even the latest Paris fashion felt-and-feathered hat she wore didn't touch the coach ceiling. But the feeling didn't last long.

The coach swayed as the fat conductor-shotgun-guard mounted the wagon. She settled in, her back to the forward seat, as she knew from many coach journeys that she'd likely get less road dust if facing the rear. She was feeling smug. Her brother, Ryan O'Rourke, had been falsely imprisoned in the Prescott jail—his relationship to her had been unknown by the locals—and was now heading north with their cousins all the way to Montana where he'd be far from those who'd wronged him and likely would again if given the opportunity. He'd escaped just ahead of a slathering lynch mob, so she had good reason to be smug.

No one but her family knew her as Kathleen O'Rourke, an Irish lass; rather, they knew her by her stage name, Elizabeth Anne Graystone. Normally she'd be traveling with her manservant and her agent. Her agent, Horace Witherham, had parted ways with her in Denver and traveled north to take the Transcontinental from Cheyenne to the west, where he was to arrange a series of concerts in Virginia City, Nevada, then up and down California. He was not apprised of the fact she'd been summoned by the rest of her family, cousins in this instance, to assist in freeing her brother. She told Horace, in no uncertain terms, that Skeeter, her manservant and bodyguard, and she would be fine and she wanted some away time. And while away she would pick up some work in Prescott, Phoenix, and then Tucson. He feared her picking up her own work as he knew if she learned how easy it was to book her talents, she might not need him or his ten-percent commission. The fact was she knew, but didn't want to lower herself to the mundane.

Elizabeth had been trained in St. Louis, then New York, then, demonstrating an angelic operatic voice and great skill as a thespian, in London and Paris. She'd adopted the English accent as it suited those who paid her handsomely to appear and hid the fact she was Irish. The Irish were despised in much of the country, and signs still adorned shop windows: HELP WANTED - NO IRISH NEED APPLY.

Then she was forced to part ways with Skeeter, her manservant, protector, and now friend, as he'd taken ill in Pueblo, Colorado, and she'd had to leave him behind. He'd worked for her for a year before he divulged his true name, John Axe. When she inquired if it was a family name, she was sorry she'd asked as he revealed he never knew his family and the name was given to him by a plantation overlord who admired his slave's use of the implement.

As Skeeter was not along for the trip, she was, as always, protected by the shiny 1870 Hopkins and Allen .32 caliber nickel pocket revolver with her initials carved on the mother of pearl grips, and, when so adorned, by the six-inch hatpin securing her chapeau—this one a bright affair adorned with Chinese ring-neck pheasant feathers.

It was just as well Skeeter had stayed behind, as she'd not wanted to involve him if things went wrong. Negros were still presumed guilty in most states and territories, even the north. It was emancipation in name only. Skeeter had already had more than his share of life's troubles, being born a slave, escaping north from Alabama to Carolina, then north again on the underground railway, and not unscathed, as he'd lost a leg below the knee to a lucky shot from a slaver who'd pursued him, and nearly lost his life to the creeping green rot.

The size of two normal men, Skeeter handled a peg leg—from six inches below the knee—just fine and had been adorned with self-hand-carved one fitted with a donkey hoof when Elizabeth first met him. It was a cause of much amusement to those brave enough to laugh at the huge man. After he proved his worth she'd invested in a new prosthetic—a booming business since the Civil War— and he now moved as if his lower leg was still attached and sported boots so if you didn't know of his infirmity, you'd think him complete.

She'd made friends with a colonel from nearby Fort Whipple, near Prescott, who'd favored her with a wire informing Skeeter of her schedule. The military had the wire off and on, when the red man hadn't cut it for the hundredth time.

Skeeter was to meet up with her in Tucson…God willing, for he had recovered from the consumption that had hospitalized him in Pueblo—with her insistence and generous payment to the hospital. The doctor had told her that Prescott would be a fine place for Skeeter, as tuberculosis did not favor a dry clime, or almost anywhere in the Southwest…when he was fit to travel.

If ever.

Chapter Two

***

She grimaced as a large, bearded man in grease-stained fringed buckskins, which reeked of sweat and to-bacco, and a floppy-brimmed hat seated himself beside her and reseated his hat on his head. She noted his holstered revolver, but that was not unusual in these parts. What was unusual was the smaller gun, Derringer size, clipped into the inside of the crown of his hat. She only caught a flash of its nickel finish, but it was plainly a belly gun if in an unusual place. Tobacco dribble stained his graying beard and a cut of chaw protruded from a pocket. He was a slovenly man, but obviously careful.

Then, another man of equal girth but in a nar-row-brimmed hat and the rough canvas pants of a miner squeezed in beside him, forcing her up against the open window, which could be covered with a canvas, should the dust become intolerable. The second man shoved a well-smoked amber-hued meerschaum pipe in his mouth and began puffing away. She decided she'd be pleased when the Concord was whipped to a breezy trot.

She sighed deeply, wishing she'd worn her split leather riding skirt, soft calf-high deerskin boots, and full silk blouse, rather than button shoes and a skirted dress with petticoat, gloves, and a cotton blouse buttoned to the throat. Bustles were coming into fashion, but she was far too wise to let fashion dictate to that degree when facing a long arduous journey.

The planned route was much flatter than the shorter route through Black Canyon. It would take them west, then south and slightly west for almost seventy miles to Wickenburg before turning southeast and driving another seventy to Phoenix.

Neither of the first two passengers had bothered with a polite "howdy," and three more crowded in across from them, facing front. The first, directly across from her, was scarecrow thin, tall with a medium top hat and bony knees that pressed up against hers and cradled a cane between them. She hadn't noticed him limping. To his credit, he tipped the top hat to her. But then, to her chagrin, he pulled a cheroot from a pocket, struck a Lucifer on the window sill, and lit up. Next to him settled in a rotund young man with peach fuzz on his cheeks, a full head of dirty blond hair as askew as a porcupine under a bowler hat. He almost quivered with excitement and she concluded it was his first trip on public accommodation. She guessed him for a clerk. Thankfully when he reached into a pocket, he came up with hard candy, not chaw, and popped it between two large lips and began sucking away.

The last to board was a Spaniard, or Mexican, in *calzoneras,* light colored trousers with a stripe of black and bright silver conchos spaced down the outside seam. His linsey-woolsey shirt was full sleeved, and he showed a tuft of black chest hair at the neck, matching a mane of black hair protruding, but nicely coiffed, under a flat-brimmed black hat with small silver conchos adorning its band. He was hawk-nosed, but handsome. She smiled demurely as he reminded her of a handsome Spaniard who'd played the fantastical Spaniard in a run of Shakespeare's *Love's Labour's Lost*. She played the Princess of France who caused him to forego his oath to forget women for three years. She and the Spaniard were very close, until she discovered he had a wife and three children in Toledo.

All but the young man wore pistols—that showed—and the Spaniard, in addition, sported a long-bladed knife in a scabbard shoved into a red sash, tied at the side with tails a foot long. She thought him not only handsome but stylish.

She was a little surprised to see another four men mount the top and boot of the coach, obviously what she knew were known as "hangers-on." Two of them appeared to be Mexican, one wore the striped shirt of a sailor, the fourth heeled boots and was likely a horseman, probably a drover. She had trouble imagining them still attached after many miles. She knew they'd be stopping to change the six-up of horses every fifteen miles or so. Maybe the hangers-on would have some time to rest, or maybe their destination was only the first division stop or somewhere in between.

She heard the whip crack and the coach jerked into a swaying lurch.

The Spaniard thrust his head out the window and looked fore and aft, then was the first of them to speak. "No escort."

The man with the pipe spoke up for the first time. "They're on a mission to New Mexico. That damned heathen Victorio killed five bluecoats and is on the prod all over the territory. They hope to intercept his band rumored to be heading this way."

The scarecrow cleared his throat and offered, "There's been no Indian trouble on this route for two years. The stage has been hit by those who call themselves knights of the road nearly every month, but no savages."

"Knights of the road?" Elizabeth asked.

"Road agents, thieves, scoundrels," Peach Fuzz added. "A gang of hooligans who've preyed on the stage and horsebackers, but only when they had no Fort Whipple escort…like we are glaringly short of now. Them brazen fools call themselves knights of the road. I heard Bob Brazelton was seen out at Iron Springs. He's a bad one. Been known to shoe his horse backward so pursuers figure him headed south when he was riding north." And he stared at Elizabeth a moment, then his jaw went slack. "You're Miss Graystone. Miss Elizabeth Anne Graystone."

She nodded and gave him a tight smile. "I knew that," she said, then laughed.

Chapter Three

***

"Damned if you ain't that songbird," Buckskin said, turning to eye her.

"Sir!" Scarecrow chastised him.

"No offense meant," Buckskin said, and backhanded some chaw spittle away. "I was there night afore last. Dang if you don't sing better than a mockingbird."

"No offense taken," Elizabeth said, then added, "I guess that's a compliment. I've heard some mockingbirds sing true opera, some imitate crows."

That made all the men laugh, and she decided this might not be too bad a trip after all.

"How about like an angel, lady? That better?" Buckskin said, then added, "My handle is Beauford Polkinghorn, Miss Graystone. Happy as a pig in mud to make your how-de-do."

Again, Elizabeth laughed, and gave him a nod, then looked across at Scarecrow, "And you, sir?"

"Maxmillian Preston, down from Chicago, offering the world's finest farm harvesting implements—"

Not interested in hearing a drummer's whole spiel on

his catalog, she moved her gaze to the young man sucking on the candy. "And you, sir?"

He palmed the ball of hard candy, and cleared his throat, then through a dumb grin offered, "Alexander Buttonworth...friends call me Button. Recent graduate of Illinois Normal on my way to Phoenix to take a position—"

And she eyed the Spaniard. "And you, sir?"

"*Señora* Graystone—"

"*Señorita*," Elizabeth corrected.

"*Perdona*, do you know the term, *haciendado*?"

"Yes, sir, I do. You are the *señor*, the owner, of a hacienda, and rancho, I presume."

"*Sí*, I raise fine horses and a few cattle. Don Mateo Jose Santiago at your service. I, too, was fortunate to hear your concert. My compliments, *señorita*."

"Thank you, Don Mateo."

She looked about the buckskin man who'd introduced himself as Beauford Polkinghorn to the man on his far side, who looked to be a miner. "And you, sir, if I may?"

"You may," he said, removing the pipe from a face lined with mutton-chop sideburns flanking a nicely trimmed van dyke beard and mustache. "Sam Johansson, miner."

"Miner?" Polkinghorn said with a guffaw. "Johansson here owns the Lynx Creek silver mine as well as one over near Jerome. I guess you could say he's a miner. Where's them fancy city duds you've taken to wearing, Sam?" Then he eyed the Spaniard and laughed. "And ol' Don Mateo here...a few cattle! He done lost count years ago of how many cattle he has on that small country he owns."

Don Mateo merely glanced out the window, modestly saying nothing.

Johansson was silent for a moment, eyeing Polkinghorn, then answered. "I'm not visiting the bank or the territorial courthouse today. I'm traveling, and don't care to have the world know my business."

Polkinghorn guffawed again. "Well, la-ti-da, Sam. Sorry I spilled the beans."

Then Johansson ignored him and focused across him to Elizabeth. "And I was blessed to enjoy your angelic voice and recitals, Miss Graystone. In fact, last year I was equally blessed to hear your New York concert."

"Well, hot damn and la-ti-da again," Polkinghorn said again, slapping his thick thigh.

"Polkinghorn," Johansson said, his voice now with a hard edge, "you have a limited vocabulary and should consider laying aside the expletives when a lady is present."

"Expletives?" Polkinghorn mumbled.

"Execrations, denunciations...swear words, Polking-horn."

Polkinghorn turned to Elizabeth. "No offense meant, ma'am," then back to Johansson. "You and I will talk about them excretions and dumbnations some 'nother time soon." His tone was as hard as Johansson's.

Elizabeth decided a closed-in coach was no place for a fist or gunfight, so spoke up quickly. "Gentlemen, I was not in the least offended by Mr. Polkinghorn's slight vulgarities, after all I am in the theater...but I appreciate Mr. Johansson's concern. Now, what is it you do, Mr. Polkinghorn?"

"Why, little lady, I go from here to there and use my wits to get by. I may trap some skins or shoot some critters to skin and jerk. I even been knowed to pan a little color now and again."

"How fascinating." Then she asked the group at large. "Gentlemen, I've never made this trip. Is it a long coach ride all the way to Phoenix?"

Johansson cleared his throat. "I have business in Wickenburg and Vulture City nearby. I have a room there and if you'd care to layover a day and complete the rest of your journey day after tomorrow, you're welcome to my very nice room."

Again, before she could answer, Polkinghorn interrupted. "By God 'ol la-ti-da Johansson knows how to get things done, don't he?"

Johansson sighed deeply, then gave Polkinghorn a tight smile. "You know, Beauford, I believe I'll take you up on that conversation you suggested. But let's wait until we get Miss Graystone safely ensconced in more comfortable accommodations."

"Suits me, Sam," Polkinghorn said, and leaned over Johansson and spat a stream of tobacco out the window, then gave him a grin. "Damned if it don't suit me."

Elizabeth sighed deeply, then decided to tough it out. "That's very kind of you, sir, but I'm scheduled into Tucson soon and might as well get there and rest up."

Johanson nodded. "Open invite, if you change your mind. I can bunk with friends if you do so."

"Thank you, sir. So, where do we stop first?" Elizabeth asked, slightly on edge again as Johanson and Polkinghorn were exchanging glances like a pair of cobras.

"We rest an hour," Johansson said, turning back to her, "at Iron Springs, where you can get a good cup of coffee or tea and some of the finest pie in the territory. But just to rest and water the team, then it's on to Skull Valley where the team is changed. Another stop and change at Miller Creek, near Peeples Valley. Then Martinez Creek trading post and inn, and well after dark into Wickenburg."

"And the stop there has accommodations?" she asked, "Should I decide to stay over."

This time Maximillian Preston, the drummer, spoke

up. "There's an African lady who runs Trinidad House, fine food in the French tradition. You'll think you're in Paris. She keeps immaculate rooms with a potbellied stove in each. It's my favorite stop on this whole southwest tour of mine."

"And I'll be able to find accommodations?" Elizabeth asked.

"I have a reservation, Miss Graystone, and if there is not a room available, I'd be honored to surrender mine."

"Well, I couldn't—"

"No, I insist."

"You are a gentleman, sir. I'll dedicate a song to you and Mr. Johansson at my upcoming concert in Phoenix, if I decide to stay over...or even if not."

"Obliged. My pleasure, ma'am."

She admired the ivory handle on the cane, carved as a duck's head. "Beautiful work...your cane, I mean."

"Thank you. I acquired it in Canada."

"We're stopping?" Elizabeth said as she was pressed to the back of her seat.

"Too soon," Don Mateo offered. He started to stick his head out the window, but a Winchester barrel caught him on the cheekbone and he jerked back inside. "Road agents," he mumbled, then added, "a tree down across the road."

Chapter Four

***

He was interrupted by the roar of a shotgun, and the coach rocked as the shotgun guard tumbled from his perch, and they heard the fat man hit the road with a thump.

Elizabeth's stomach roiled and knotted. For the second time in almost as many hours, a man had died a violent death too near her.

"My God, I never shoulda—" young Alex, the fledgling teacher, muttered.

"Shut up," Elizabeth snapped, then eyed each of them quickly. "Are you gentlemen going to stand for this?"

Before they could reply, the robber stuck his face up to the window in the door. "I know you fellas are heeled to the teeth, but before you pull and go to committing suicide, you should know there are a dozen long guns trained on this here cheese box you're all caged up in. If'n you open a door to dismount, they take to ventilating the cheese box with y'all in it. If you don't chuck them sidearms out into the road, they take to ventilating the cheese box. I figger a dozen shots each from a dozen rifles will pert near shoot y'all in every place y'all got a place to be shot. Now, if you agree, go to chucking weapons through them windows."

Elizabeth studied him. Not a face she knew, but one she'd remember. He had a patch over his left eye, a pocked face, and she guessed was at least half Indian or Mexican. She almost smiled to note he had a monocle on a leather tie hanging from around his neck and resting on his chest. Even with the monocle in place, he wouldn't look like a European aristocrat. She almost laughed at the thought, but remembering the twenty ten-dollar double eagles in her reticula, the two hundred dollars in paper money there, and more seriously the five thousand dollars, or more, in jewelry she had hidden the false bottom of her valise, sobered her.

Luckily, she'd visited the Miner's and Stockman's Bank in Prescott and deposited over four hundred dollars from her concert in Prescott's Tempest Opera House, then drawn a draft on it and mailed it to her bank in New York.

But even more valuable than the money, and the rest of her jewels, was a broach given to her by her father, an ivory carving of the image of her mother. It was carefully packed with the other jewelry. She would clamp teeth and merely rue the loss of all, but the broach.

She glanced out her side of the coach and saw two men making their way down out of the pines, one carrying a Winchester, one a shotgun.

Then to her surprise, another face appeared only a foot from hers. She wondered how he'd crept up to look in, then realized he'd climbed up. He was a dwarf, a Mexican dwarf, who was a small version of the pock-faced road agent with the monocle. Tiny in stature, but large in ugly, with a head too big for his body, he wore a huge sombrero almost as wide as he was tall.

"*Buenos días*," he said, with a cackle, then jumped down.

The man with the monocle snapped at the dwarf. "Enano, get away in case we have to ventilate the coach." And the little man scampered off with a giggle. He wore a revolver with its muzzle hanging nearly to his knee, even with a sawed-off barrel. Then Monocle addressed the hangers-on. "You trash, two-finger them revolvers, drop 'em in the dust and go to running off into the woods. 'Cept you, Tolliver, of course."

The two Mexicans and the man with the striped mariner's shirt jumped down and hotfooted it into the woods. The fourth man, dressed as a drover, walked over and joined the speaker. Obviously, he was one of the road agents.

"Firearms, now," Monocle said. Then a firearm roared and blew a hole from one side of the coach through the other but near the roof, not missing the tall men by more than two inches. Before the echo died, firearms began flying out the coach windows. Elizabeth did not reach for her revolver. Few would suspect a woman to possess one.

All five men passengers leaped from the coach as ordered.

Only then did a barrel-chested, black-haired, blue-eyed Anglo step out of the underbrush and saunter forward. He held a shotgun, loosely, at his side, and wore a double rig of Colts. One under his left arm in a shoulder holster, butt down, one at his right side.

"Step out," he ordered. Elizabeth waited until they'd all unloaded, then fished her little five-shot revolver out of her reticula, quickly hoisted her skirt, and slipped it into her garter, high on her thigh. Only then did she reopen the door and carefully turn and back out of the coach. Johansson, the miner, or mineowner, stepped forward and helped her down, barely beating Don Mateo to the task.

"My oh my, bless my rotten Welsh soul, if it ain't Miss Graystone, the English songbird," the barrel-chested man said, his voice triumphant. He removed a broad-brimmed hat and with a sweep of it and an exaggerated bow, bent at the waist.

"And you are?" Elizabeth asked, brushing her skirt and eyeing the big man.

"Llywelyn Bowen, at your service, Songbird. You may call me Louie. All my dear friends do."

"Then I'd guess you're seldom called Louie, if ever."

"Why, ain't you the sassy one. You must'a pocketed a pile from them Prescott concerts. Do I have the pleasure of pattin' you all over to discover that coin, or would you prefer to produce it ladylike?"

"I have my traveling money in my reticula, but most of it was banked in Prescott, you'll be sorry to learn." She glanced at the others, from man to man, then returned her gaze to the one who called himself Louie. "You've been rude, sir. An introduction to the rest of your fellows?"

"He's dead as a stone," Tidwell, the whip, interrupted, before Louie could answer, as Tidwell rose from kneeling at the side of his bloodied shotgun guard. The coach gun, a short-barreled double-barrel twelve-gauge, lay nearby, and Tidwell glanced at it, then back at Louie.

Louie laughed. "Go ahead, driver. There's six of us—"

"You said a dozen," Elizabeth challenged.

"That was Mangas tolt you that lie, not me. And, yes, it was a lie, but a half dozen plus one of us'n coulda shot y'all to fodder, so it don't matter."

"Do not try it," Elizabeth advised the driver. Then she turned to the others, "With Mr. Louie's word, I suggest we hand over the valuables and he'll let us go on our way." Then she turned to Louie. "Do I have your word on that, Mr. Louie?"

"So, you consider yourself my dear friend?" he replied with a laugh.

"Should you give me your word to let us go on our way, less our valuables, I'll consider you an unfortunate acquaintance...at best."

"If that there's the best I can get, then I agree." Then he turned to Tidwell. "Pick yourself a couple of these galoots to help, and spread them valises and whatnot out on the road and fish out that strongbox."

Tidwell motioned to Polkinghorn, the trapper, and Johansson, the mineowner, to come help, and began unstrapping the boot.

Louie turned back to Elizabeth. "I surely wouldn't want you to go to thinkin' I'm the rude one, so, that little fella is Enano, and tougher than a javelina twice his size. The dog-butt-ugly old boy with the funny glass for his eye is Mangas Zaragoza-Jones, half-breed son of Colonel Matias 'No-Prisoners' Jones, recently of the Confederate Texicans under Kirby Smith. Now a happy *haciendado* of Mexico. That skinny boy with the eagle feather in his sombrero band is Flaco and the other skinny one is Alfonso...Fonso to us...Flaco's half-Apache half-brother. And Tolliver who was your fellow passenger is a recent escapee from that hellhole over at Yuma."

Elizabeth could only shake her head disgustedly. "And a fine band of fellows you are."

As Louie was expounding on the group, Enano and Mangas rifled through the baggage, while the Comacho brothers herded all but Elizabeth over to the side of the road and had them set on their hands on a blowdown ponderosa pine.

The dwarf, Enano, and the hanger-on, Tolliver, reached

deep into the boot and came up with the strongbox. Elizabeth was surprised at the obvious strength of the little man as he handled his share of the load with seeming ease. They hoisted the box, and dropped it into the road. Dust flew from under the slamming iron-trimmed box. The man with the patch and monocle, Mangas, was quickly on the box with a small sledgehammer and chisel. With only three blows, the hasp sprung aside with the lock still closed. Mangas looked up with a wide grin as he viewed the paper money and coin in the box.

Elizabeth watched the men going through the bags carefully, and happily they dumped her small case with the false bottom, but didn't discover her jewels or spare stash of cash.

The knot that had been her stomach began to relax, then she screamed, as Beauford Polkinghorn came out of his hat with the Derringer and blew a hole through Flaco Comacho's skinny neck.

Violent death number three!

Chapter Five

***

Elizabeth had seen her share of violence, having sung in many a saloon before she moved up to opera houses after her training in London and Paris. She saw her first man killed at the tender age of sixteen, a man knifed in the chest during an altercation. She'd learned one certainty along the way...to stay alive, stay out of the line of fire.

The instant she saw the trapper jerk his pocket gun from his hat, she dove under the Concord, as all Hell hit like the conclusion of Beethoven's Fifth, and filled the air with gun smoke and its acrid, olfactory scorching odor.

Sam Johanson dove for Flaco's brother, Fonso Comacho, knocking him flying but then took the load from a barrel of Louie Bowen's shotgun to the chest and, with a shower of blood and gore, was blown backward over the log. Fonso came up with a sidearm and fanned three shots into Beauford Polkinghorn's chest, and at the same time Beauford fired the second barrel of his Derringer into Fonso's gut. Fonso grabbed for his stomach with one hand and stumbled away to flop on his butt near the log, and yell, "*Carumba*, by all that's holy, I'm shot."

Don Mateo Jose Santiago, followed Elizabeth's example and dropped behind the ponderosa pine blowdown, and remained out of sight. He had been disarmed of his sidearm but still wore a large Arkansas sticker in his red sash...but wisely didn't pull it.

Maximillian Preston, the slender drummer, was on his feet, and to her surprise he jerked on the duck's head and a ten-inch hidden blade appeared, flashing in the sunlight. He made the mistake of charging Louie with the blade raised overhead. Too long a time as he might have made it to his target had he merely lunged forward. The dwarf, Enano, shot him in the back, dead center. Blood splattered across Louie's face and he laughed as he backhanded it away, then wiped it on his trousers.

Alexander Buttonworth, the fledgling teacher, and Oliver Tidwell, the whip, leaped up and ran back into the woods, and the one-eyed Mangas Zaragoza-Jones popped his monocle in place and proved its worth as he raised his Winchester, which he'd laid beside the strongbox, and fired a single shot. Buttonworth hit the forest floor hard, kicked a few times, flopped from his stomach to his back, screamed "Mama" twice, then was still. But the old whip disappeared into the forest as Mangas was levering in another shell.

"Shall I run his ass down?" Mangas asked Louie.

"Hell, the old bastard is likely to have a heart attack and die trying to run up that mountain. He ain't shooting at us, so to hell with him."

Elano the dwarf, with his Colt in hand, had sprung over the log and was sitting on the Don's chest, holding the muzzle at Don Mateo's throat, and the stylish Mexican Don wisely didn't twitch.

Tolliver, the drover-attired road agent who'd posed as a hanger-on passenger, had bent to drag Elizabeth out from under the Concord at the same time other weapons were being discharged. He had that lascivious look she'd seen on so many men in her life. To his surprise, she'd palmed the Hopkins and Allen and shot him between his wide and very surprised eyes. He spun away and hit the road on his stomach, unmoving.

Looking back, she saw the legs of Louie Bowen and Mangas Zaragoza-Jones striding her way, and quickly slipped the little five-shot back into her garter, flinching a little as the barrel was hot. A shotgun, even one with only one barrel still loaded, and a Winchester, and two skilled shooters were too much firepower for her to challenge. Not to speak of the dwarf who was only twenty yards off the road, with the wicked looking sawed-off revolver in hand.

When they bent to look under the Concord, she appeared as wide-eyed, fearful, and harmless as a schoolmarm and held both her hands out to demonstrate clearly that she was unarmed and harmless. She carefully climbed out from under the coach and stood before Louie, brushing the road off her skirts, repositioning her hat. She was silently praying no one had seen her dispatch Tolliver, as the coach was between the deed and the other robbers.

While adjusting the hat, she had the urge to pull the six-inch hatpin and drive it into Louie's chest, but figured the rotten road agent had a heart so small and hard she'd miss or be unable to penetrate.

She decided to bide her time. He had given his word he'd let them go on their way.

A little surprised the black-haired Welshman didn't shove her up against the coach and fish under her skirt for the revolver, she continued to play the frightened little lady.

And it was working, so far.

Louie smiled broadly and touched the rim of his

hatband, and only then she realized he was the same man who'd killed another in front of the Palace Saloon, and given her a grin and the touch of his hat brim as he'd galloped by.

She was sure both Polkinghorn, the trapper, and Johansson the miner, were as dead and gone as yesterday. Maximillian Preston was face down in the road, unmoving. Buttonworth, the teacher, had gone down hard and lay unmoving. Tubby, the guard and conductor, hadn't twitched since he hit the road with a belly full of buckshot. Flaco Comacho, shot through the neck, was twitching in the pine needles but she was sure he would never rise again. Fonso Comacho, Flaco's brother, was now on his back, moaning, holding his stomach but off to the side. It was likely not a deadly wound, if he was lucky enough to have had the little Derringer bullet miss a bowel. Tolliver, with a .32 between the eyes, bled little and moved not at all.

Tidwell, the whip, was last seen disappearing into the woods. He, the Don, and she were the only ones left of passengers and crew still on their feet. Tidwell and the hangers-on seemed long gone.

"Let him up, after you slip that pig sticker outta his sash," Louie instructed Enano, who dismounted, taking the Don's Arkansas toothpick with him.

Don Mateo rose to a sitting position, keeping his hands flat on the ponderosa.

Louie waved Enano over and snapped, "Go watch the woman." Then to Mangas, "Get the valuables into saddlebags and them passenger bags."

The little man padded over to where Elizabeth leaned on the coach, taking in the bloody scene around her. Mangas began stuffing coin and paper into bags, and other items they valued, including the passengers' firearms.

"You pretty *gringa*, for a *gringa*," Enano said with a broad brown-toothed grin.

"Thank you," Elizabeth replied. "And you are a handsome man," she lied.

He grinned stupidly.

Louie bent over Fonso, his hands on his knees, studying the wound.

Then he sighed. "You ain't gonna be riding, old pard."

"Then…" Fonso said, and gasped before continuing. "Then load me in the coach and let's haul for Mexico."

Louie laughed. "Hell, Alfonso, we wouldn't get past Wickenburg afore horsebackers ran us down and hung us from the nearest saguaro. Besides, that tree we felled is holding us back, and afore we could clear it the law dogs will be on us."

"You ain't leaving me here, *chingaso*."

"Better you get a *medico* in Yuma Prison than die on the road, buzzard food."

"If'n you think you're leaving me here, you're *loco* in the *cabeza*."

"Fine, old pard. That fine-looking palomino of yours is only a hundred paces down in the pines. How about you hustle on down there and mount up."

Fonso tried to rise, but winced and had to lay back.

"See what I mean, *amigo*,' Louie said.

"Then fetch my *caballo*, cut out my share of the loot, and I'll rest up here afore I ride off."

Louie was quiet for a moment, then laughed, but only with the mouth, not the eyes. He gave Fonso a sardonic grin. "You ain't earned no share until the job is over. And the job ain't over until we're back in Mexico with the law dogs far away."

Fonso's Remington revolver was only two feet from his

right hand, but it might as well have been two hundred as he tried to reach for it.

Louie had the shotgun hanging at his side and didn't have to rush as he lifted the muzzle and cocked the hammer at the same time. As he was only four feet from Fonso, the blast only holed his near side the size of a twenty-dollar gold piece, but exited the other side of his rib cage the size of a coffee cup. Fonso didn't have time to curse Louie as his blood and innards slathered the pine needles under his now silent body.

Enano left Elizabeth's side, and ran to Fonso. "He was my *amigo*," the little man groaned.

"Now you have a third the loot, not a seventh," Louie said, and Enano looked up, the furrows between his eyes went away, and a broad grin covered his face.

He stuttered, "One-third better than one-seventh, right?"

Elizabeth had heard about the horse, tied in the forest below, and slipped around the coach, hoisted her skirts, and ran downhill.

"Watch him," Louie yelled at the little man, motioning at Don Mateo, then he hotfooted it after the women. As he passed Mangas he yelled over his shoulder. "Gather the goods!"

He caught Elizabeth easily before she was halfway to the tethered horses.

Mangas yelled after him, "Do not injure her, she will warm our beds."

Jerking her around, Louie gave her a grin, then said, "You tired of our fine company?"

"I had to try," she said, gasping a little from the run.

"You will be mounted soon enough. You will pack one small bag. You will change into something more suitable for riding horseback."

"You said you would leave us after you had our valuables."

"I lied, little songbird. Does that surprise you?"

"It would surprise me if you were honorable."

"I had planned to escort Mr. Johansson down to Mexico, knowing his family would pay handsomely for his return... but, alas, not so much for his cold corpse. You, and Don Mateo, will have to suffice." He chuckled as he added, "You're together likely not worth a full thunder pot, but I'll give it a go."

"You, sir, are a lowlife son of a whore."

"Aw, little songbird, you have found me out. Now climb in that coach if you're a bashful one and change your attire. We ride for Mexico."

Chapter Six

***

Elizabeth was pleased she had some privacy, par-
ticularly since it allowed her to transfer the garter and the
Smith and Wesson without being discovered. Although
nearly all women rode sidesaddle, she had long forked
a saddle like a man, wearing a split leather riding skirt
and near knee-high boots with a mid-height riding heel.
The bad news was the loss of her beautiful Paris gowns
and accouterments, the good, she was able to select the
valise that hid the false bottom and her money, jewels, and
particularly the broach that had belonged to her mother.

Her few moments of quiet time while changing her
clothes gave her time to reflect on what she'd done, and
consider the consequences. She'd seen plenty of violence
in her few years entertaining in saloons, and traveling
the world, but today was the first time she'd done more
than jam a hatpin into some arrogant or aggressive male.
She'd killed a man with a few grams of lead between the
eyes. It both sickened and excited her. Defending yourself
and yours was a responsibility she'd been taught from the
time she was old enough to understand, and in the final

analysis you could only depend upon yourself to do so. And you must have both the courage and the capability to act. She decided she wasn't sorry she'd done so, only sorry it was necessary.

As she was repacking, she glanced up to see Louie leaning over Tolliver, the man she'd shot. He glanced back at Enano, who was moving their way with Don Mateo in the lead, his hands on his head, Enano's Colt poking him in the back.

"Enano, did that fat slovenly fellow fire that little Derringer twice or more?"

"I no know," Enano said with a shrug.

"Must have, this ain't no .44 caliber hole in Tolliver's noggin. That's a hell of a shot with a Derringer from thirty paces."

"No know," Enano repeated.

"Okay, cut them six mules loose. A good Christian fella like me wouldn't leave 'em harnessed up to starve. Keep two to pack. Use saddles from them other mounts. We'll hang our goods off'n them. We'll turn the extra horses out. If they follow, fine. If not," he shrugged.

"Yes, *Jefe.*"

"I'll take over here. You fetch their weapons. They'll each bring near a ten-dollar gold piece down Mexico way." Then he turned his attention to Don Mateo. "Keep your hands atop your pate." Then to Elizabeth, who was exiting the coach. "Why, ain't you the stylish one. I'll bet you ran them poor old foxes over in John Bull land."

"With the best of them," Elizabeth said.

"It's a long hot ride, Songbird, but you're gonna love Punta de Piedra o Puerto Peñasco."

"Where?"

"Puerto Peñasco. Ain't no opera house there. Fact is,

ain't but six stools and two tables in the cantina. But it's got the most beautiful sunsets on earth coming across the Sea of Cortez, particular if'n you got a bottle of pulque in one hand and a *señorita bonita* under yer arm."

"How far?" Elizabeth asked, with some trepidation.

"Only two days, two full hard hot days, south of the border. God willing and the creek don't rise." Then he laughed. "We'll be there in six or eight, God willin' and the afore-mentioned creek don't rise. Course there ain't hardly a trickle twixt here and there, so that ain't much of a threat. We'll be blessed if there's a water hole."

We won't be there at all, she thought, *if I get a chance to stick my little revolver in your ear*, as Louie led her, dragging her by the wrist. The ugly Mangas followed, with Don Mateo behind and Enano behind him, prodding him with his Colt. *There's only three of them and two of us, if the Don is worth his weight in piss and vinegar, we'll have their heads on a pike soon enough.*

Louie led her to a tall palomino with a Mexican rig, the large horn bound in caramel-colored leather, a few silver conchos on the skirts, and a horsehair braided bridle, reins, and latigo. But Louie slipped the bridle off and stuffed it into the palomino's saddlebags. He did the same with his shoulder holster. Then he uncurled the lead rope.

"You won't be showing off them fox hunting skills till we're far from anywhere and you running off would be inviting dying with a tongue all swolled up and your skin a blisterin'. I'll lead 'til then."

"Nice horse," Elizabeth said, through clamped teeth.

"Ol' Alfonso Comacho done willed him to you...least for this trip. You stay forking him, quiet like, while we pack up. You act up again and you'll find your wrists bound like the ol' Don there."

They loaded Don Mateo into the saddle of a tall dappled grey, tying his wrists behind him. The bridle was removed from the gray, as had been done from the palomino, and its lead rope tied to a pine sapling.

The three remaining road agents went to work, packing the two mules from the Concord six-up, with the loot they'd gathered and sharing the load of a packhorse they'd left with their riding stock. They used leather satchels, passenger's luggage, as panniers, and tied her bag atop on one of the mules.

Enano rode a full-size pinto, at least fifteen hands, and had a drop stirrup that allowed him to climb into the saddle, then he hooked up the longer step-stirrup, tying it up out of the way with a saddle lanyard. All of them sported saddle holsters for their sidearms, but Louie kept his shoulder holster in place.

Mangas rode a sixteen-hand red roan, and Louie rode a chestnut that was as beautiful a mount as Elizabeth had ever seen, but she held her comments thinking how she'd enjoy riding it back after she and the Don had figured out how to leave the three owlhoots for the vultures.

For the first time since the robbery began, she had the opportunity to speak to Don Mateo, low so the others couldn't hear. "We will survive this, Don Mateo."

"*Sí, señorita*. Don't mistake my caution for cowardice. All things in their own time."

She merely nodded, content she had a compatriot.

In moments, five of them set out. Louie in the lead, dragging Elizabeth's palomino. Mangas followed, leading Don Mateo's mount, and Enano brought up the drag, leading a pack string of two mules and a horse.

***

"John," Doctor Quinton, in his white coat, ad-dressed John 'Skeeter' Axe, across his wide walnut desk, twirling a long handlebar mustache as he did, "we're not sure you had consumption, tuberculosis, and think… hope…it is only a bad case of bronchitis. If so, it was one of the worst cases I've had the displeasure to treat." Then he chuckled and continued. "You've got a chest the size of a small horse, so maybe it had more surface to infect."

"Sir, what would that bron…bron stuff be?"

"An infection of the lungs and bronchial tubes. Not nearly so…so fatal as consumption."

"So, can I pack up my satchel and catch me a stage south?"

"Let's give it one more night. Fact is the Southern Overland Mail leaves south at 8:00 AM. That'll give you time to eat and make it to the express office. I notice you haven't coughed once since you've been across the desk?"

"No, sir. Not all the day long."

"I doubt you're contagious."

"That mean I won't be passing it on to the next fella?"

"That's what it means."

"You got enough coin to pay my debt?"

"Miss Graystone left more than enough. Fact is you've got the better part of two hundred dollars coming back to you."

"That include breakfast in the morning?"

The doctor laughed. "Fact is, that's part of my diagnosis. Kitchen tells me you've been eating enough for two the last couple of days. A sick man seldom eats a trough full. So take advantage of Consuela's good grub one more time before you say *adios.*"

"I don't s'pose you heard from my employer?"

"Last word I got was the wire I showed you. She finished

in Prescott and was heading for Phoenix and then Tucson."

"Well, sir, I thanks you and all the ladies. Y'all treated me real fine. As a man of color, I find y'all to be special good folk."

"You're a special fine fellow, no matter your color, John. Fact is we could find a place for you with our maintenance and grounds staff—"

"Thank you, sir. But I'm obliged to Miss Graystone."

"I understand. If I'm in the office come time you leave, stop by and let me give you a handshake."

"Proud to, doc. Proud to do so."

Chapter Seven

***

Louie Bowen reined up and turned back to Eliza-beth. "Sun's 'bout to duck below the mountains. We done made good time, considerin' we're dragging y'all."

"What's that smoke up ahead?" Elizabeth asked. "A hot meal, I hope. Maybe a bath?"

"You're sure enough spoilt, Songbird. That's the Skull Valley Trading Post. But you ain't going in to palaver with Mr. and Mrs. Potter. There's a spring a mile down this hill where we'll camp, then I'll ride in and see if Mrs. Potter's got any extra. Dang sure she does as the stage was scheduled to make a quick stop."

"Mr. Bowen, if I'm badly handled, my family will be remiss to pay a farthing for me. You're not going to leave me with that Mangas and Enano are you?"

Louie laughs. "Them relations of your'n don't give me a response I like, next I send one of them pretty fingers of your'n along and see how they take to that." He laughed again. "I guess you'd like me to cut the Don loose to watch over you while I fetch somethin' better than beans and jerky?"

Elizabeth didn't bother to answer.

"Fact is," Louie continued, "they'll not partake of any of our valuables, and what you're carryin' in them leather britches is sure as valuable as all the gold coin we stolt, less'n I cut 'em loose, then you'll wish a pack of wolves had at you."

"A pleasant thought. How do you plan to contact my family, and the Don's?"

"You'll tell me where, and I'll send a message on the wire from Wickenburg or somewhere has a key. The Don's little 'ol hundred-thousand-acre land grant is only two days ride from Punto Peñasco. We'll carry a message to his kin."

"The only address I can give is the Conner's, general delivery, Bozeman, Montana. But odds are, Mr. Bowen, they are already on the trail to find you and tack your hide to the outhouse wall whence they'll tear off a piece in lieu of a corn cob. It's kin you should worry about, but not the Don's. You harm me and—"

"Yeah, yeah, yeah, that's what they all say. I ain't scared of no bunch of John Bulls."

"My kin are all Irish, Bowen. And they eat the Welsh and the English for a tea-time snack. All fighting men, not long out of the recent unpleasantries, and have sent many a red man, and a few deserving Anglos and Mexicans, to their happy hunting grounds since. That was my brother left a bunch of faces in the mud in Prescott, and he and my cousins haven't gone far. They'll track you to Tierra del Fuego and tack your hide to that outhouse wall I mentioned, you so much as break one of my fingernails."

"I wondered…you with that hair black and shiny as a raven wing and them blue eyes as pretty as a gemstone, you're damn near pretty as a Welsh maiden. All that considered, you have proved to be as sassy as a murder of damn crows and it's tiring. You keep yapping and I will leave you to Mangas and the dwarf."

"You've been warned."

"As have you, lass. Now let's get to camp."

They made a quick camp, under the cover of a few narrow leaf cottonwoods, staking out all but Louie's beautiful chestnut near the spring, but far enough they didn't litter it with their waste.

Don Mateo was tied with his back to a tree trunk. Elizabeth was surprised he had not said a word for hours, nor did he complain now. But the dark eyes beside that hawk nose were also hawk-like, surveying and taking in every detail before he lay his head back and closed them.

A rock circle for a campfire was already in place, as that spot near the spring circled by fresh grass was obviously popular. Before they were finished hanging canvas pack covers as makeshift tents, Louie swung easily into the saddle.

He snapped at the two he was leaving behind. "Do not touch the woman unless she tries to flee. Touch her and you answer to me. I would enjoy having half or all our treasure." He awaited a reply, got none, but seemed satisfied and continued. "We are short on coffee and I need to replenish my shotgun shells and .44s if the post has some in stock." And he gigged the chestnut and cantered off.

The one-eyed man watched him go, then replaced his monocle, smiled hungrily, and sauntered her way while loosening his belt.

Elizabeth was adamant. "Stop right there, Mr. Zaragoza-Jones!"

"And why should I?"

"Are you not the son of Colonel Matias 'No-Prisoners' Jones, who served valiantly under Kirby Smith."

"I am, and damned proud of it."

"I know something of those brave men, and know Jefferson Davis welcomed them with 'Texans. The troops of other states have their reputations to gain but the sons of the defenders of the Alamo have theirs to maintain.' Isn't that true?"

"My *padre* was among them."

"And you would soil the memory of those brave southern men by raping an innocent woman?"

"Aw, *señorita*, I am an *hombre* of Mexico now, and my grandfather fought at the Alamo," then he chuckled, "Only on the side of the victor. And are you not a woman of the stage, who's been in many a saloon and bawdy house?"

"I am, and an honorable one, and still a maiden." She lied. She'd lost that status at the age of eighteen. But the lie might serve her.

"Ha, you'd lie to keep a stallion like me from having my way with you? Even though afterward you'll sing my praises to the heavens. You amuse me."

Elizabeth yelled to Enano. "I thought you were a man among men. If he has his way with me, I will take my own life and be no good to anyone. I'm worth a great deal to you all, but not soiled. And Louie will kill you, if you cost him money."

"I could be your defender, Miss Lady," Enano said, but she wasn't convinced.

"I thought," Elizabeth sighed, "your courage was much larger than your size."

Unfortunately, Enano glanced away, then moved to re-pin the stock.

Mangas swelled his chest, and stepped closer. "Louie is Louie but I am Mangas Zaragoza-Jones, who will take much killing. Many have tried."

But after he crowed, he backed away and refastened

his belt buckle, and Elizabeth exhaled a breath she'd been holding. Another bridge had been crossed.

Mangas gave her a start as he spun and strode back to her. "Do you do more than chirp, Songbird? Do you cook?"

"Of course, kidney pie is my specialty," she lied. She'd eaten, but never cooked kidney pie in her life.

"Then I suppose you can slice and fry bacon. My water bag is half filled with well soaked beans. As we have the spring, no reason to save the water. There's watercress near the spring. You know watercress?"

"Of course."

"And red peppers in the mule's pack. Many peppers *por favor*."

"I'll make two batches."

"Fine, we have a deep skillet and a pot."

He spun again and walked away and she let out another deep breath. Then called after him, "Don Mateo needs to be freed for a while. You have him tied so tightly he could lose a hand."

Mangas walked over and leaned with his hands on his knees, eyeing Don Mateo. "*Es, verdad, haciendado?*"

"Is true. And I need to have a few minutes behind a bush."

Mangas laughed, then yelled to Enano. "Hey, shorty, the great man has needs just as the rest of us. Draw your weapon, stay at least ten feet from him while he does his business, then escort him back and I will retie him." Then Mangas loosened the Don's bonds and with his sidearm in one hand, helped him to his feet with the other.

Enano drew his Colt and followed a few steps behind as the Don moved into the underbrush.

The Don tried nothing, and she was glad to see him return with Enano following ten feet behind.

She had the beans boiling as Mangas began to retie the Don.

"Leave a hand free," Elizabeth commanded, "so he can eat, unless you want to spoon-feed him."

Mangas gave her another evil laugh, then growled, "I will loosen a hand when you are ready."

By the time the beans were softened and the bacon fried, Louie returned, carrying a muslin sack. He dismounted and smiled as he removed a deep-dish apple pie and sat it on a log. "We dine in style," he said, then added, "I must return the dish on our way by in the morning." He walked to his saddlebag and removed a wide-brimmed sun hat with a scarf tie. Then to her, he handed it over. "Noticed that fancy lid of yours blew away sometime back. Wouldn't do to have the Sonoran sun bake your brain like this pie."

It was hard to get out, but she did. "Thank you."

As they ate, Louie made assignments. "Mangas, you will take the first watch. Wake Enano," he pulled a pocket watch from a pocket with its gold chain, and continued, "at one AM. Enano, you are number two. Wake me at four and I'll take the morning. If I catch either of you sleeping, I will cut your throat from ear to ear."

Louie unrolled Fonso's bedroll for her, but it was all she could do, even remaining dressed, to climb between the wool blanket and wool serape that made up the bedding. She feared lice or bedbugs, or something worse. But the desert night had dropped fifty degrees and she quickly relented.

And she was surprised how quickly her mind went blank.

Then she was roughly awakened with a calloused hand over her mouth.

"No sound, Songbird," Louie whispered, his mouth so close to her ear she could feel his hot breath.

Chapter Eight

***

She was sure he'd crept up on her with evil intention, then when he made no move, listened. The sound of distant hoofbeats. And she realized the moon was down. It had been hours since she'd crawled into Fonso's filthy bedroll.

"Don't scream. You yell out and I'll turn you over to Mangas and that nasty little man." He loosened the hand from over her mouth.

"Night riders," she whispered.

"Likely a posse. Them damn fools didn't waste no time."

"Maybe they like their songbird," she said, more than a little derision in her tone.

"That there Hatch Stinman, territorial law dog, is trying to win his spurs for a run at territorial governor. But he ain't got the sand to take on the likes of me."

"Sounds like he's eager to give it a try," Elizabeth muttered. She'd met Territorial Marshal Hatch Stinman, and was impressed with him. Her brother, Ryan, had spoken fairly highly of Stinman before he'd ridden out with kin headed for Montana. Then she'd met him in the hotel restaurant and he'd seemed more than a little interested in her. But then more than a few men were. Stinman had engaged her in a long conversation, wondering why she was traveling alone. She'd informed him of her booking agent's trip west and of her man's, John 'Skeeter' Axe's, unfortunate illness and hospitalization in Pueblo. And she was more than a little curious when the nice-looking marshal not only listened intently, but took some notes. She had high hopes he was as good at his job as Ry, her brother, had indicated. And she was doubly surprised that the lawman wasn't on the trail, trying to ride down her kin as her brother had escaped the Prescott jail. If, in fact, Louie was right and the distant hoofbeats were a posse and the posse was led by Stinman. It could just as likely be someone running from the law.

"Tryin' ain't doin'," Louie said, sitting up and firing up a small cigar.

The hoofbeats faded, several horses, likely on the road they'd left to head for the spring. With no moon up, it was a wonder they could even stay on the road, much less track. Obviously, they'd missed where she, the three road agents and Don Mateo had turned off for the camp spot. She said nothing in reply, so he continued.

"Tryin' sure as Hell's hot ain't close to doin'. And the three of us can take down a half dozen who don't know we're laying for 'em. I rode out of the Skull Valley post heading southwest, telling them I was on my way to far off Yuma. Looks like I ain't getting' my four-bit deposit back for the pie pan." He stood and stretched. "We'll fight shy of the post come light." Then he laughed. "Hell's fire, we'll likely be on the trail of the posse. Ain't that a hoot."

***

With the sun barely peeking onto the plains to the east of Pueblo, Skeeter was dressed. Ever since he'd been employed by Miss Graystone, she'd been giving him the education that would have been considered a crime when he was enslaved. He could now read and write, at least enough to get by while traveling. She'd left him with a copy of *An American Dictionary* by Noah Webster, a heavy volume, and a copy of *The Mystery of Edwin Drood*, by Charles Dickens, and he'd passed his time reading and learning new words. He wasn't a fast reader, but he was a conscientious one and never let an unknown word pass.

He left a note for Dr. Quinton, thanking him for all he'd done. He'd settled his bill of fourteen dollars the night before, explaining that he was out to catch a stage and would be leaving even before breakfast. The kitchen had provided him with a jar of canned apples and half a loaf of bread, and told him they were sorry to see him go, but happy he seemed well.

He worried he'd have to buy a horse and make his own way south, as the coach would be costly, but then he'd been informed he could take the new narrow-gauge Denver and Rio Grande to El Paso, Texas, then the Texas and Pacific west to Tucson, if he had the coin. So, he headed for the train station. He still had one hundred and eighty dollars, and was confident it would do.

The agent at the Denver and Rio Grande didn't seem too pleased to make Skeeter's acquaintance.

"You got the fare, boy," the officious little man asked Skeeter, who was first in line when he removed the board blocking the passageway in the counter top iron fence separating his office from the waiting area.

"Well, sir, how would I know till you tell me how much it be?"

"Big as you are, I should charge you double."

"I only gonna take up one seat, sir."

"No, boy, you're not. You can ride in the baggage car. But we don't cater to negros in our tourist cars and sure as the Devil is likely black, not in first class."

Skeeter narrowed his eyes, but kept his comment to himself. "So, what be the fare?"

"It's two cents a mile on our fine narrow-gauge."

"I need to pick up the Texas and Pacific."

"That would be Las Cruces, New Mexico. And," he studied a chart on his side of the fence. "Five hundred three miles. Let's call it an even ten dollars, since you'll be with the baggage."

"And the fare for other folks in the passenger car?"

"Ten dollars and six cents."

"Well, sir, I'm proud you saved me six pennies for some hard candy." Skeeter thought about reaching through the little opening and seeing if he could drag the skinny agent through, but let himself calm down and reached in a pocket, and to the seeming surprise of the agent, removed a five-dollar gold piece slapped it on the counter.

After the agent overcame his surprise, he asked, with a curious look, "What's your name, boy?"

"John Axe."

"The hell you say. I got a wire here for a John Axe. My runner was to take it to the hospital, but now that you're here…." He walked away to where an operator sat by the chattering key, and gathered up a paper and returned, passing it through to Skeeter.

"How long?" Skeeter asked.

"How long is the wire. Can't you read…of course you can't—"

"I reads just fine. How long till the train leaves?"

"Two hours. On her way down from Denver, and on time. By the way, you might want to take some grub. You ain't gonna have access to the dining car."

"How much more from Las Cruces to Tucson?"

"You'll have to take that up with the Texas and Pacific. Move along now, there's white folks behind you."

Skeeter gave him a nod, and moved over to a bench, and plopped down to read the wire. He presumed it would be from Miss Elizabeth, and was very surprised to see it from a Marshal Stinman of Prescott.

Miss Grayson missing. Stop. Likely kidnapped
by road agents who robbed our stage and
now headed south. Stop. Deputy Josh Clemmons
of my Prescott office will be kept informed. Stop.
She indicated she was to meet you in
Tucson. Stop. Suggest you head here. Stop.

Skeeter quickly headed back to the agent's window the instant an older couple stepped away.

"What?" the little man snapped.

"Change of plans. I gotta go to Prescott, Arizona Territory."

"Ain't no train to Prescott. You'll wanna go south to Albuquerque on the rail, then see if you can join up with an Army outfit headed to Fort Whipple. That's your best bet."

"Then I'd appreciate a refund of the difference."

"We ain't in the refund business, boy."

Skeeter merely glared at him for a moment, laid his massive clenched fists on the counter, then in a very low voice so he couldn't be overheard, said, "Sir, my mama taught me to be fair to all folks. And I sure would hope your mama taught you the same. I guess my ticket will be just as good tomorrow as today, so I could wait somewheres in the shadows until I see you wandering by and we could talk on this some more…or you could just be a fair gentleman and refund me the difference."

The agent reddened in the face until Skeeter worried he was having an apoplectic fit, but then he pulled open his little cash drawer. "It's six dollars and seventy cents to Albuquerque. Here's three dollars and three dimes. We usually charge a ten-percent refund fee—"

"Well, sir, I want to tells you how much I appreciate it. I'll put a good word in with the man above, should you give me your name?"

"We're fine here. How about you wait on the bench outside."

Skeeter tipped his hat to the man and spun on his heel and headed out. He couldn't help but smile. He'd taken a risk. Had the agent called the sheriff there likely would have been hell to pay.

But his bluster had worked. This time. He'd have time to go to a nearby mercantile and get himself a sack full of hardtack, some hard candy, maybe a sausage, and a couple of bottles of sarsaparilla. And, particularly if he was going to be horseback on the road, another box of .44s for the Remington stuck in his belt.

New Mexico and Arizona territories had been immersed in Indian trouble.

Chapter Nine

***

The hangers-on from the stage, and the whip, Oliver Tidwell, had, afoot and limping, stumbled into Prescott in the early evening. Tidwell had pulled the Arizona Territorial Marshal, Hatch Stinman, out of the Palace Saloon. It was past eight PM before Hatch had put together a posse and a crew to gather up the bodies and the coach.

He left his deputy, Josh Clemmons, in charge of the jail and law enforcement, recruited Anthony Azevedo, a rotund piano player from the Sundown Saloon, who he knew would last about twenty miles before he begged off, and Filo Parkenson who was a city dude and would be right behind Azevedo. Aleandro Sanchez was a trail tough vaquero and would probably outlast Hatch. Rory Maxwell and Harrison Higginbottom were hard sorts and had been vigilantes at one time, and both had recently returned from trying their hand at ranching near El Paso. The latter two and the vaquero would likely hang until they wore through the iron shoes on their mounts. It was the two dollars a day the territory was paying and the two dollars a day offered by the Arizona Territorial Express making a more than average wage of four dollars a day. And a five-hundred-dollar reward bonus to each man if all or even part of the missing money was recovered. There would likely be a generous dead or alive reward offered when word came from Express Company headquarters, and they had time to print posters.

They had ridden hard, most of the night before reining up at the Skull Valley Trading Post. There were no lights on in the place, nor at the farmhouse a hundred yards distant out in a clump of cottonwood near the trickle of a creek.

Hatch dismounted from his lathered sorrel and loosened his animal's cinch, then turned to the others, "Y'all loosen them cinches and let your animals blow whilst I roust the Potters and rustle us up some coffee and biscuits."

He couldn't help but smile as the fat piano player, Azevedo, nearly fell from the saddle. Filo Parkenson didn't need the money and Hatch wondered why he'd signed on. He looked about as beat up as Azevedo as he eased himself to the ground, then rubbed his butt cheeks with both hands. Sanchez, Maxwell, and Higginbottom made easy dismounts, and all quickly cared for their mounts, loosening chinches and even removing bridles.

"A trough?" the vaquero asked.

"Round back. I'm heading for the house. Water my animal if you would."

Hatch strode off toward the house, with the sun just beginning to lighten the sky behind the six-thousand-foot peaks between Skull Valley and Prescott to the east. Mr. Potter, likely awakened by a couple of barking mutts, was on the front stoop with a lantern in hand by the time Hatch reached the house.

Potter held the lantern up as Hatch approached.

"Well, howdy, marshal. What brings you all the way

out our way?"

"Good morning, Mr. Potter. Breakfast for six, if Mrs. Potter's in the mood. We been riding all night."

"Posse?"

"Yes, sir."

"Hunting who?"

"A big barrel-chested fella and his chums. He's suspected of shooting down a customer of the Palace and if that wasn't enough, looks like he robbed the stage before it got to Iron Springs."

"Well, sir, you're a little late to the party. He was here last evening. Alone. Sold him pie, some shotshells, and a box of .44s."

"Notice which way he headed."

"More than noticed. He rode out southwest, saying Yuma was his next stop. Then all the way to Los Angeles to buy hissef a saloon and bawdy house. 'Course he didn't say that with Mrs. Potter about."

"I'll bet. However, murderers and thieves been known to prevaricate when it suits them."

Mr. Potter laughed. "You don't say. I'd never guessed. Nice enough fella. But he was alone so far as I could see. How-some-ever, I doubt if he bought that wide-brimmed lady's sun hat for his own use. He had on a fine wide-brimmed light brown hat. He bought an apple pie and put down a four-bit deposit on the tin. Hope he don't return it as I can buy two tins for the four bits."

Hatch nodded, not surprised, then continued, "Don't worry, he ain't coming back, particularly if he's spotted our stock. A poster from El Paso said he's known to bunk with *banditos* from south of the border. There was no talk of Mexico?"

"Not so much as a whisper."

"We'd better move along if you'd be kind enough to wake—"

"She was pulling on her cookin' dudes when I left the upstairs."

Hatch had to laugh again as he gathered up his sorrel from the Mexican. He led him around to the hitching rail in front of the post and thought for a moment thunder had rolled down out of the hills...but it was Azevedo, sprawled on a bench on the post porch, snoring like a military drum roll.

***

Louie jerked on the lead rope and waved the palomino and Elizabeth up beside him as they flanked the Skull Valley outpost, staying far up on the mountainside to the east.

"When are you going to let me rein on my own?" Elizabeth asked before he could say anything.

"I tolt you. When we get out on the Sonora sands and all you'll get by runnin' off is a swolled tongue, dead horse, and a prayer you'd never left us'n."

"And how long is that?"

"We'll be campin' south or west of Wickenburg then two more days to hot sands and lava flows. Just ride easy and enjoy the view."

"Ha," Elizabeth managed.

"How about you sing us a little ditty as we wander south."

"I wouldn't sing for you louts if you paid a hundred dollars each for a seat."

Louie chuckled. "I'll tell you what. I'll bet you a kiss you'll sing for your supper tonight, or you'll be one hungry songbird."

"Ha," she managed again, and swung a doeskin booted foot over and kicked Louie's sorrel in the side so he leaped forward and her mount was again being dragged by a taut lead rope. Louie just laughed.

As before, Mangas followed her, leading Don Mateo whose wrists were tightly bound to the saddle horn, followed by Enano, leading the string of two horses and the mule.

Louie laughed, then turned and spoke over his shoulder. "You ain't got any in that black hair of your'n, but I'm gonna sing you the song anyhow." And he began with a voice that surprised her, particularly acapella,

"Darling, I am growing old,
silver threads among the gold
Shine upon my brow today
Life is fading fast away.

But, my darling, you will be, will be
Always young and fair to me
Yes, my darling, you will be
Always young and fair to me.

When your hair is silver white
And your cheeks no longer bright
With the roses of the May
I will kiss your lips and say.

Oh! My darling, mine alone, alone
You have never older grown
Yes, my darling, mine alone
You have never older grown."

"Dang, that's all I remember," he said, then seemed to be thinking hard.

She was impressed with his voice, if untrained, but wouldn't give him the satisfaction. "Not bad, for a toad frog."

"Yeah, but I didn't charge you no dang dime."

"And you charged what it was worth…no dang dime."

"You'll sing for your supper, lass. Or wish you had…."
And he gigged the sorrel into a single foot.

Chapter Ten

***

Skeeter was impressed with the smooth ride and speed of the narrow-gauge rail train, after it pulled up the long grade over Raton pass and they entered New Mexico Territory. If the train had a tender car, as many did, they wouldn't have had to stop every ten miles for water and wood. Even so, he figured they were averaging thirty miles per hour. Even with the stops they were scheduled into Albuquerque come early morning, two AM, well before daylight.

The baggage handlers were decent fellows as well as was the guard. The baggage car also carried a safe, which seemed to need guarding.

One of the handlers was a negro boy from Louisiana, Rolondo, who'd been a cook in the army and had served at Fort Whipple near Prescott and at Fort Verde, so as they rode along with the car door wide open and their legs dangling down, he filled Skeeter in on not only Prescott but the trail there from Albuquerque and gave him the name of a Black, Paul Fitzpatrick, who'd long been a freedman and who had a small farm, was a skilled blacksmith, and raised horses, outside of the small town. He assured Skeeter he'd be treated fairly by the smithy.

He was sure Skeeter would find a good mount and tack there for less than fifty dollars. And it had to be a good mount as it was nearly four hundred miles of rough, dry, Indian country between Albuquerque and the first real civilization at Fort Verde, then another forty some to Fort Whipple just northeast of Prescott. All of it savage Indian country.

Every five minutes an image of his employer, benefactor, teacher and friend, Elizabeth Graystone, flashed through his mind. If some no-account lowlife scum had hurt her, he would wade through them like scythes and sickles through wheat, and leave less than sheaths behind. His mouth went dry at the thought of a gang of stinkin' road agents using her badly.

"Wha' the matter?" Rolondo asked.

"What you mean?" Skeeter replied.

"You got them hands so fisted up yer gonna poke them nails clean through your ol' pink palm."

Skeeter relaxed his fists and rubbed his palms together. "Just thinkin' 'bout a friend of mine who's needin' a bit of help."

"A lady friend?" Roland gave him a wide grin.

"Fact is, she is, but not the kind you're thinkin'. She's a white woman been kind to me." He reached down and rapped his knuckles on his wooden leg. "She got this chunk of tree to finish off'n this leg."

"You got a wood leg?"

Skeeter relaxed with a laugh. "I do. And I'm gonna shove it where the sun don't shine, when I catch up with some fellas I hear done her wrong."

"I got me some kin in Prescott. You mind I come along?"

Skeeter studied him a second, then shrugged. "Sure enough as you done know the way. But you gots a fine job right here?"

Rolondo glanced over his shoulder to make sure he wasn't overheard, as the train sang along on the rails at nearly forty miles an hour. Then he leaned closer, "If you think four bits a day and a hard cot in a baggage car a fine job, then I'd like to know what a lousy one might be."

Skeeter laughed. "Well, sir, then I'll enjoy the company of a fine guide and a second gun on a dangerous trail."

"More dangerous for some than for others."

"How so?" Skeeter asked.

"I done lived with them Apaches, the Yavapai, for more'n a year. I talk that jabber of theirs right fine. So long as that's the only tribe we run across, if'n we run across even them, we'll be gooder than a hen in a pea patch."

"How'd it happen you used to live with the Indian?"

"I run off from a plantation down in Texas, and run and run until the Yavapai come on me in the desert, near dead. They got me right, and over the next year I returned the favor when a few of them come down with the Cholera."

"Then you'd be handy as a pocket in a shirt. Proud to have you along. I'm buying me a Winchester in Albuquerque—they got one in stock. You gots a firearm."

"Sure do. Scattergun."

"Then I'll do the long work, you do the short."

***

Just as the stars began to show they camped out-side of Wickenburg in an eight-foot-deep wash, more than a hundred feet wide, lined with screw bean mesquite. It was a dry camp, but they'd passed a brackish water hole only a couple of miles back, watered the stock, and filled their water bags.

When Louie and Mangas untied Don Mateo's hands from the saddle horn, but left his wrists bound, they dragged him from the saddle and left him on his back in the sand. Elizabeth slipped from the saddle and strode over to check Don Mateo's wrists, both bleeding from the cutting rawhide they were bound with.

"You filthy pigs!" she snapped at Louie and Mangas.

The one-eyed man stepped forward and slapped her hard, spinning her around and dropping her to her knees.

"*Carumba*," yelled Enano as he ran up behind Mangas and hit him hard in the spine with the butt of his revolver. Mangas screamed, dropped to his knees, and grabbed his back with one hand but whipped out his revolver with the other, cocking it as it came. He spun around to face Enano, both with muzzles pointed at the other, from only three feet apart.

"Go ahead, you dumb donkeys," Louie said with a guffaw. "Shoot each other. I'll enjoy spending your money."

Both of them cut their eyes to Louie, then back.

"You hit Miss Lady again, I shoot you in the *cojones*," Enano said with a growl.

"Shoot him now," Elizabeth said, adamantly, as she wiped some blood from the corner of her mouth.

"How about," Louie said, his tone more serious, "I shoot all of you'n's."

Don Mateo sat up. "Go to hell! A real man does not mistreat a woman." Nearly the first words he'd muttered since climbing from the coach.

"We will be in Hell," Louie said, "in two days. The Sonoran sand and lava are close enough to Hades to make you wish you'd never sinned and pray forgiveness. Now, *amigos*, holster that iron before we have an accident.

You two watch each other and our charges while I ride into town and get us enough to get us to Punta Punesco. *Comprendes, amigos?*"

"I need some bacon grease for the Don's wrists," Elizabeth said.

The two of them slowly re-holstered their weapons, and only then turned from facing each other. Enano hurried to the mule's pack, pulled a small folding knife from his pocket, and reached and sliced some fat from a side of pork belly, then hurried back and handed it to Elizabeth. She gave him a smile and a nod, then began dressing the Don's wrists as best she could with them still bound.

"Untie him," she said to no one in particular.

"Will not happen," Louie said. "Late tomorrow maybe, maybe next day, if we reach the organ-pipe cactus near the border." Then he eyed both Mangas and Enano. "If I'm not back in two hours, the wire has reached Wickenburg and I'm in the hoosegow. Y'all tie them back to back and come in shootin', you got it, *amigos?* And if I return and find you've molested the songbird, or allowed either of them to fly, you will wish I'd been captured. *Comprendes?*"

Both Enano and Mangas gave him a nod, and he swung onto the saddle as if he hadn't just ridden nearly forty miles, and gigged the still willing sorrel toward town.

Mangas yelled at him as he gave heels to the sorrel. "*Amigo*, remember, the posse may be ahead of us. Be aware of the smell of law dog."

Louie gave him an acknowledging wave over his shoulder, then gigged his mount into a canter. Now, with luck, the town marshal is drunk or out hunting javelina, or in the brothel with his favorite soiled dove.

With luck.

Chapter Eleven

***

Much to the chagrin and moans of his posse, Hatch Stinman passed the sign on the crossroad turning east to Wickenburg. Another sign pointed south to Vulture City, only ten more miles. They'd passed a rider on the trail and questioned him about where he'd come from and who he might have passed on the road. He reported four horsebackers just outside of Vulture City who'd swung well off the road as he approached. He didn't think any of them women, but it was hard to tell through the mesquite and ocotillo.

Wickenburg, founded by the German who'd discovered gold to the southwest, had the wire, and a smart road agent wouldn't risk riding into a town with a marshal who might have just received a wanted notice. Vulture City was founded by the German in '63 due to a gold and silver strike, and was, to date, the territory's largest producing mine. Both Vulture City, at the mine site, and Wickenburg were growing with new miners, city folk, and drovers from scattered cattle operations. But Vulture City was a company town, and independent folks flocked to Wickenburg so as not to be under the German mineowner's thumb.

Louie obviously wasn't a smart road agent, or he was brazen and overconfident. The sorrel would normally be single-footing, showing off for the city folks, but he was beat from the long ride, and plugged along like a plow horse.

A waxing moon was just over the low mountains to the east as Louie plodded in. Few businesses had lights in the window, other than three saloons and a mercantile. Pianoforte and banjo music floated across the hard-packed road.

Louie had heard they had a new marshal in Wickenburg. A young fella, so the word was.

Tommy Torrel Thompson had only been on the job for two weeks. His blonde wife, Martha, and two youngsters, both as brindle-topped as their young father, were happy with their new abode: A little whitewashed ranch house with a pair of peach trees and some berry bushes, shaded by a pair of stately cottonwoods. The most dangerous thing he'd been faced with in the first two weeks on the job was breaking up a fight between a pair of burly Vulture Mine mud grubbers, and they'd been so drunk neither of them had landed a punch. Saturday night was the only night he wasn't expected to work, unless rousted from home by trouble, but he was tipped generously by the saloon owners for keeping the peace so it wasn't so bad. Tommy had to whack one of the miners aside the noggin with his brand-new Merwin & Hulbert .44 nickel-plated revolver to get his attention, and had let them both go the next morning, before Tommy joined his family at church. Sheepish, sober, and hungover they offered their apologies, and walked out now seeming to be best friends.

Thompson was making his last rounds of the day and had stopped in Willingham's Mercantile and General Store for some salt and sugar for Martha. He fancied a new hat he'd seen in the window and was in front of a looking glass, adjusting the wide-brimmed sand-colored chapeau on his full head of red hair when Louie tied the sorrel out front and wandered in to stock up before the long ride across the Sonoran sand and lava.

He stopped abruptly when he saw the badge shining on the waistcoat of the man admiring himself in the mirror. Louie shook his head slightly…just his luck.

Louie brazenly ignored him and walked to the counter.

"Howdy, friend," Mark Willingham greeted him with a smile, resting his ample belly on the edge of the counter.

Louie touched his hat brim. "Need a side of bacon, five pounds of beans, five of flour, two of coffee beans…I favor Arbuckle's if you got 'em…a box of .44s, and a pound of hard candy."

Marshal Thompson was studying Louie in the mirror's reflection, and as Willingham went to work filling the order, turned and strode his way. Louie was not to be taken by surprise and was watching him in the reflection of a glass-fronted cabinet behind the counter.

The counter had a stack of peach tins, just the right size to fill a hand, and Louie picked one up and pretended to be reading the label.

"Llywelyn Bowen," the marshal called out. Then repeated, "Louie Bowen!" Louie could see the redheaded man had his hand resting on the revolver at his side.

Louie didn't turn, or acknowledge the calling of his name. To do so would be to confess who he was.

The marshal reached out, a questioning look on his freckled face, and tapped Louie on the shoulder. Louie turned with a grin.

"Howdy," Louie said, and knocked the hat flying as he smashed the peach tin into the side of Thompson's head.

The young marshal went down like a sack of potatoes.

"Hey," Willingham yelled, and Louie spun his way, drawing his Colt in the same motion. "Don't…!" the grocer yelled, extending his hands palms flat out.

"You stand very still, grocer man, while I relieve this foolish young fellow of his firearm."

Louie gave the grocer a nod, then spun back and, almost point-blank, fired a round into the unmoving marshal's chest. The merc rocked with the shock of the load and acrid smoke filled the room. Dust motes floated down from the rafters, and the corpulent grocer stood with mouth hanging open, his chin tripled, and eyes wide, face going white as the bleached flour he sold.

"No, no, no," Willingham finally managed.

"Finish my order, fat man," Louie demanded, centering his Colt on the grocer's chest, as he bent and retrieved the marshal's sidearm. He admired it for a moment. "Dang if this ain't one of them new Merlin's or Merwin's or some such. Fancy weapon for a young lawman."

The fat grocer was gasping for breath so hard Louie thought he might pass out as the gunman walked to the door and looked in the direction of the three open saloons. In two of them, men stood behind the batwing doors, and looked out as if curious where the shot came from, but neither pushed through.

"Hurry it up," he snapped at the grocer, and walked back to the counter.

"Here you are," the fat man said, pushing a loaded muslin sack across the counter.

"What's the cost?" Louie asked.

"Just go."

"Aw, hell man, you got costs. How about," Louie raised the muzzle of the Colt and fired a shot into the fat man's chest, then muttered, "a half ounce of hot lead." The shot slammed the grocer back into the glass cabinet behind, which smashed and sprinkled his protruding belly with shards from overhead as he sunk to the floor, sitting, gasping, holding his chest with both hands. He had the shocked look of a man who thought he'd never die.

Louie gazed down, making sure the merc proprietor was finished, then crossed himself—after all he was Catholic—and muttered. "Always try and remember Father, Son and that sneaky ol' Holy Ghost."

Louie started out with the sack over his shoulder, then spun back and sunk to a knee beside the unmoving marshal and snaked his revolver out of his holster and shoved it into his belt. He chuckled as he bent and unfastened the pin holding the lawman's badge to his waistcoat, opened the pin, and shoved it into the marshal's nose. "Now, don't you look fine! Your ol' mama would be proud." He guffawed at the sight of the brass badge centering the young man's face, then he hurried out, tied the sack behind his saddle, and swung up.

A half dozen men had filtered out of the saloons, so Louie re-palmed the .44 and snapped a high shot off at the lighted window of the nearest saloon. It shattered and men scattered in every direction, including back through the batwings.

Louie gigged the sorrel, spinning him away between the mercantile and a tonsorial parlor next door. The sorrel kicked clods out behind for a leap or two. When out of sight of the men at the saloons he reined his mount back to a brisk walk and toward the wash where they'd camped.

It was a quiet camp when Louie rode in about ten PM, but not for long. He went from bedroll to bedroll, found Elizabeth on her face with wrists bound behind her, and knelt and untied her.

She was spitting mad. "That bastard Mangas bound me. Then turned his back on me and relieved himself on the ground. He's a heathen and a filthy scoundrel." She turned away as she wiped a tear from her eye, not giving them the satisfaction of seeing her wet eyes.

Mangas, who he'd awakened first, defended himself. "The bitch tried to slip away. I let her go behind that bush for privacy and she tried to skedaddle."

"Aw, Songbird," Louie said with a low laugh, "if you try and run, we will only run you down. And maybe run you over with a *caballo*. You will be too sore to run again."

"Why do you awaken us?" she asked, changing the subject.

"We move on."

"In the dark?"

"*Sí*, in the dark. We will pass Vulture City then no more lawmen. In four or five days we will be enjoying the sunsets in Puerto Peñasco with a bottle of pulque while enjoying the music of a fine guitar and the voice of an angel. And not you, songbird. Another angel."

"Your wife?"

"Ha, there is no woman who could tame me. Just a *carino*."

"*Carino*?"

He laughed again. "Sweetheart. I have many. Some cook, some clean, some for more intimate purposes. You will beg to become one." When Elizabeth ignored him, he continued. "Some are fat, some *mucho flaco*…but my favorite are like you. Not chubby, not boney, just right. The closer to the bone, the sweeter the meat, but too close is stringy." He laughed. Still, she did not respond. "Tend to your bedroll. We ride out in ten minutes."

"You did something wrong, in Wickenburg, right? So, another posse is on our trail?"

"Ha, all I did was pin the pretty brass badge on their marshal." Then he roared with laughter. When he collected himself, he added, "Right or wrong, we have supplies. Now, move."

As she was packing, she made note of his pulling a revolver she'd not seen before out of his belt and stuffing it into a saddlebag on his animal. The Morgan was lathered up, and she wondered how it would fare with another hard ride, and little or no rest.

With luck, the chestnut would collapse under him.

Chapter Twelve

***

Horace McCabe was Marshal Tommy Torrel Thompson's brother-in-law, Martha's older brother. He'd been in the States less than ten years, and shortly after landing in Boston Town on a hot July day, he found himself in the Union II Corps and two months later in Miller's Cornfield, at a place called Antietam, where the crop was turning from green to brown, near the Hagerstown Turnpike, under the command of Major General George McClellan. He was a Scotsman, a clansman, and had seen his share of blood and battle. But it had been nothing compared to what roared around him. He awoke, after a near cannon strike, two days later in a hospital with two fingers of his left hand gone, and a broken forearm and shin bone. It was enough to get him sent back to Boston. He arrived two days after President Abraham Lincoln issued what was called the Emancipation Proclamation.

He would learn after the war that the battle of Antietam—called Sharpsburg in the South—would be the most bloody of any one day in the war, with over twenty-one thousand men dying. He began to believe he was one of the lucky. Two thousand more would die later from their wounds.

He sat out the rest of the war, working in a foundry, casting cannon, happy to be near the heat of a roaring furnace and out of the heat of battle.

Then McCabe went west, and, after a year, with a letter extolling the virtues of the desert, convinced his younger sister, Martha, and her new husband, Tommy, to join him.

Now, as he stood and stared down at the corpse of his brother-in-law, he wondered how he would tell his little sis of their loss and knew that he must ride out in pursuit of his murderer as soon as he informed her, even before they could plant young Tommy in the rocky desert soil.

Horace found it hard to breathe, and wondered if he'd ever take a full breath of air again. He wouldn't. Not until Tommy's killer was fodder for the worms.

As soon as he returned from consoling Martha and the girls, he packed his dappled gray and stopped from house to house, beating on doors as it neared midnight. Finally, he had three men who said they'd ride with him to avenge the young marshal's murder, and that of the jolly old fat man, the grocer, who'd carried the tab of many a family in need of food and feed.

***

Paul Fitzpatrick was not happy when his barking hounds awakened him long before dawn, and even less so when someone pounded on his front door loud enough to awaken Pimento, his Jamaican wife.

"Who de hell?" she snapped as Paul pulled his boots over his long johns.

"Who the hell knows, woman. Get your feets under you and get down the scattergun. But stay upstairs. I'm going down." He grabbed up his old Volcano lever-action pistol in one hand and the lantern in the other, and quietly took the stairs.

Before he reached the bottom, a voice rang out through the thick planks of his front door. "Mr. Fitzpatrick, it be Rolondo and his friend Skeeter, here to do some horse tradin'."

Rather than open the door straightaway, the burly blacksmith-farmer-horse-breeder walked to a window and quietly swung the shutter open and tried to focus on the two figures at his front door. The skinny one he recalled, but the other was as big as one of his draft horses and unknown to him. The huge man wasn't one you'd forget.

"Don't y'all move off the stoop 'til I gets some light on." He strode over to his wife's iron stove, fished a Lucifer out of her holder, struck it, and lit the lantern, then returned to the window to set it on the ledge, turning it up to full wick. "Y'all move into the light." And he stepped back into the darkness.

They did so, side by side in the window, and Rolondo gave him a wave. "Y'all remember me, Mr. Fitzpatrick. I done swathed meadow grass for y'all only two years past."

"What the hell brings you here at this time of night? You done woke that devil woman what married me and it's a wonder she didn't shoot y'all from the upstairs window."

Rolondo laughed. "I do remember Miss Pimento and them flapjacks that would float off'n the plate."

"You're Rolondo alright. Dang if you ain't. Who be your little friend?"

Rolondo laughed again. "He's a friend, goes by Skeeter, in need of horse enough to tote him and I need something to get me as far as Prescott."

"Well," Paul said, moving toward the door, "leave your

weapons outside. I got the horseflesh; you got the coin."

Skeeter lay his Colt revolver on the stoop and both he and Rolondo leaned his long gun against the house. The door opened but only a couple of inches until the big blacksmith was assured they'd done as told. Then he swung the door wide and motioned them in.

"Put yourselves down at the table yonder. I'll fire up the stove." He fed the firebox on the big iron range then walked to the stairway and yelled up. "Pimi, y'all get decent then get down here and cook us up some Arbuckle's."

"Obliged," Skeeter said, speaking for the first time.

"Who de hell is dem rascals?" rang down from the upstairs.

"Dem rascals is customers, woman. So speak kindly of them and hurry on down to say 'howdy'."

"Humph," was the answer.

Paul returned to the table and sat across from Skeeter. "So, you needs a critter to carry you, or do you plan on carrying him?"

"Need something that's got some sand and ain't afraid of rocks and cactus. My mistress was stole by some lowlifes and I plan to ride 'em down. I also needs me a Winchester. You got one you'd part with?"

"Happens I have one too many. Got a fine '66 Winchester Yellowboy if'n you got a ten-dollar gold piece?"

"I do, if you'll throw in a box or two of shells?"

"Seeing as how you're about to ride into the jaws of hell. Now, a desert horse," Paul replied, "don't need to be a runner, but needs to be tough, steady, and long. You understand?"

"Yes, sir. I worked lots of stock, mules and draft animals when we was all under the whip."

Paul merely nodded. "I got a mule, half-Percheron,

half-devil donkey, or a Perch mare, either will do the job for you."

"You got 'em," Skeeter said, "and what will it take for me having 'em?"

Paul laughed. "It's fifty for the mule, sixty for the Perch mare. She may be in foal, don't know yet."

"And I don't know how long my quest might be, so likely the mule would be more fittin'."

"Likely."

As they talked, Pimento descended the stairs, a robe over her nightgown, her hair in a twisted towel. "Y'all are headed for the barn, I'd surmise? I'll heat up a bit of last night's stew if'n you got a mind to fill your bellies."

"Howdy, Miss Pimento," Rolondo said, whipping his hat off.

"Why, glory be, if'n it ain't skinny Rolo," she said with a wide grin. "What brings y'all back?"

"Mr. Skeeter here needs a mount, as do myself, and we need to ride on. Some lowlife fellas got a head start on us all the way over in Prescott. But we sure as shootin' got time to eat anything you'd care to whip up."

"Go on about y'all's bid'ness, and I'll get some coffee to boiling and stew to heatin', an' maybe a few them biscuits you like."

"I'd be in heaven, ma'am, afore my time."

It was midnight when Skeeter, after paying the full fifty dollars for the mule but acquiring in addition a saddle and blanket, bridle, forty-foot leather reata that had been shortened to that length by a break, pair of hobbles, picket pin, goat-gut water bag, a grain nose bag that had been smeared with enough pitch to make it waterproof as well, and old Army saddlebags, rode out on the sixteen-and-a-half-hand mule that had a neck the size of a keg and an attitude that said, "pay attention, fool."

Thanks to Miss Pimento, they had enough in their bellies and the saddlebags held enough hardtack and venison jerky to last them the hard trek to the Territorial Capitol of Prescott.

Rolondo and his little pinto horse could ride through the barn door without removing his hat or bending. But the fourteen-hand paint was desert tough, and had cost Skeeter only another forty dollars including a scarred McClellan Army saddle and bridle.

The last thing Paul Fitzpatrick said before they mounted up was a caution: "Them Apaches is on the prod twixt here and Prescott. Y'all keep a sharp eye. Them mounts you bought won't outrun 'em, but they'll charge into the devil's teeth need be. Go with God, fellas."

Chapter Thirteen

***

Marshal Hatch Stinman led his posse into Vulture
City well after dark. They stalled their mounts at the hostler,
who was likely home and in a warm bed. Knowing they'd
surely leave long before the man returned to work, he left
two silver dollars and five dimes for the three stalls and
six scoops of grain. The town's little café was closed, but
High Flying Vulture, the little mine town's only saloon, was
roaring away. Beer and sausages wrapped in tortillas and
slathered with refried beans would have to do. Hatch went
from group of men to group of men asking about four men
and a woman on horseback, but got nothing but shrugs and
dismissal from those playing faro and the wheel of chance.
He did no better at the long bar.

He gathered his men, Anthony Azevedo, Filo Parkenson, Aleandro Sanchez, Rory Maxwell and Harry Higginbottom, telling them to down their beers, and they headed
for the only rooming house in town.

Azevedo, the rotund piano player, sidled up next to him
as they headed down the block.

"Hatch," he said, with a bit of a quaver in his voice, "I

ain't going on out into the desert. This is it for me."

"Tony, you signed on—"

"You'd spend more time looking after me than chasing them fellas were I to go. I'm done in."

"Me too," Filo Parkenson echoed from behind.

"Any other chicken shits here," Hatch yelled at the others.

"I got four *muchachos* to look after," Aleandro Sanchez yelled from five feet behind them. "It ain't a matter of scared, it's a matter of no one looking after my little ones."

"Hell," Hatch said, turning and eyeing the vaquero, "ain't your oldest fourteen?"

"*Mi hija* is fourteen tall and round, but only eleven *años*."

Hatch sighed deeply. "You got two day's pay coming when I return. Don't get snake bit on the way to a safe warm bed."

"We ain't leaving now," Tony Azevedo stammered.

"So, you expect me to buy y'all a room and breakfast when you're quittin' on me? No, sir. You're off'n the payroll and the dole as of now. Make your beds under the stars and I'll have your silver when I return."

"We going on come morning?" Rory Maxwell asked. "South, I mean."

"I don't believe they came this way. I think the damn fools went to Wickenburg, so we'll head north to the cutoff after we get six hours of shuteye. I'll wake y'all at three-thirty or four. I want to be in Wickenburg at sunup."

"That's twelve miles or maybe fourteen."

"We'll grain the horses a mite more, then push hard. We'll make it, or close. If our animals can keep up the pace."

Harry Higginbottom stepped up on the rooming house stoop and caught up with the other two. "I ain't had this much hilarity since I closed myself in the privy with a skunk."

"Don't worry," Hatch said, "tomorrow is likely to be lots more laughs."

***

Louie, Elizabeth, Mangas, Don Mateo and Elano rode in the darkness for four hours, due south from their arroyo camp, four miles west of Wickenburg. They would stay well clear of Vulture, and after crossing two low mountain ranges, letting their animals pick their own way on game trails, they would be only thirty miles from the Buckeye Trading Post where Louie had long ago made friends of Emanuel Vasquez, the old man who owned the place and distilled the best pulque in Southern Arizona. After that, it was only seventy miles to the border, and another thirty to Puerto Peñasco.

Elizabeth was sore, angry, and, above all, attentive. She knew if she didn't escape soon she'd have little hope of finding her way to any sort of civilization before she died of thirst, got snake or gila monster bit, or was captured by the savages known to survive on cactus, lizards and rattlesnakes where a white man would give up the ghost after a day on the Sonoran frying pan. Apaches or Yaquis could be lying in wait behind the smallest greasewood stand.

Elizabeth yelled ahead at Louie. She and Don Mateo were still being led, and Don Mateo was still suffering with his wrists bound, "Mr. Bowen, we either stop for some sleep or I will fall from the saddle."

He glanced back. "You might fall once, then I will bind your pretty trotters to the latigo and when I finally cut you free, you will have creases that may never go away."

"And I pray the English cut the throat of every bloody Welshman."

"Ha," he said, but merely rode on.

***

It was a good thing the road out of Vulture was well traveled.

It was as dark as Satan's lair with the fires out when Hatch, Rory and Harry rode out, hoping they'd find the outlaws, the Mexican Don, and the woman still in or near Wickenburg when they arrived. They'd only been on the trail a little over a mile, when Hatch, in the lead, reined up.

"Quiet!" he snapped to the others in little more than a loud whisper.

"What?" Harry asked in the same tone.

"I heard a horse whinny. Let's get off in the brush. Could be they pulled off the trail to rest somewhere and we passed them last night. Don't shoot the woman or the Mexican."

All three of the posse pulled their long arms from saddle scabbards. Harry and Rory took the east side of the trail, Hatch the west.

It wasn't long before they heard the clomping of hoofs. More than one animal. Four or five, Hatch figured.

"How the hell could we be so lucky?" Hatch said under his breath as the riders came closer.

Hatch cupped a hand over the hammer as he cocked his Winchester to quiet the ratcheting, and slipped from the saddle. The brush was chest high and the low mountain behind him assured him he was not backlighted by what little starlight there was.

When they were no more than twenty paces, Hatch shouted, "Riders, drop your reins, raise your hands. You're under the gun on all sides."

Horace McCabe, dead Marshal Tommy Thompson's brother-in-law, realized he'd been dozing. He cursed himself under his breath when he realized he'd ridden into a trap. In his mind's eye, all he could see was young Tommy dead on the grocer's blood-soaked floor, and the grocer, equally dead, leaning, splayed, up against a cabinet, his prodigious belly covered with blood, sparkling with shards of glass.

It also flashed through his mind that he wished he'd taken more time and been more persnickety in choosing men for his posse. But reason and judgment had been melted with the heat of anger. Melander 'Lanny' Quince was a city boy, and Horace had been surprised when he said, "I'm up for an adventure," and hurried to shed his nightshirt, dress in his roughest duds, and saddled his dun gelding. Horace was sure Quince had never killed so much as a deer, although maybe he'd trapped a mouse, and so he was surprised when Lanny's Winchester, too near to his left side, roared.

Hatch's horse side-leaped away into the sharp brush, and he and horse tangled in a tall ocotillo, the spines of which caused the horse to try and shed itself of rider and cactus, doing a hell of an imitation of a porpoise, hump-backing back onto the trail. Between flashes and roars of weapons, it was all he could do to try and stay forked.

He was fifty yards down the trail before he got the dappled gray to still, shivering and blowing, but still. He could hear his horse blowing and snorting as he turned in the saddle and looked back to make sure he had no pursuers.

He slipped from the saddle, glad to realize he was not holed by one of the many shots fired from both sides of the trail. He hunkered down and started back, Winchester now in hand.

When only fifteen yards from where the ruckus started, he heard a voice yell out. "Give yourselves up. We're a duly appointed posse from Wickenburg, and you are under arrest."

Hatch couldn't believe his ears. The man who'd fired the first shot had been almost as quickly shot from the saddle and lay in the trail, gutshot and moaning. The other two had turned tail, hunkered down in the saddle, and were galloping out of sight.

Hatch took a deep breath, then yelled back. "It ain't us under arrest, it's y'all. We are a duly appointed posse from the territorial capitol of Prescott, and I'm Marshal Hatchinson Stinman."

There was a dead silence for a moment, then the voice rang back, sounding a little shocked, "The hell you say." Quiet again, then he added, "You gotta be shittin' me?"

Chapter Fourteen

***

"You rotten sons o' bitches might as well just shoot me twixt the eyes," Elizabeth said, as she threw a leg over her mount's neck and slipped to the ground. It was the first curse she had uttered in front of others in years. They were riding in a deep wash, and at midmorning there was still shade from the east bank of the twelve-foot-deep cut.

"Hey, Songbird, the way you talk you may be banned from polite society," Louie yelled at her as she stumbled into the shade and collapsed.

"Hay's for horses, and what would you know about polite society?" she replied, then added. "Shoot me dead. I'm not getting on that godawful horse until my fanny stops feeling like you've been horsewhipping me for a week."

Louie sighed deeply and reined their horses over into the shade.

"Get the Mexican down," Louie yelled at Enano and Mangas.

Enano dropped the lead rope from the two-horse, one-mule train he led and slipped from the saddle.

Mangas was leading the Don's mount, so, dropping the lead rope and dismounting, was first to his side. The Don made no move to dismount so Mangas shoved him hard. But the Don was nearly born in the saddle and a hard vaquero to dismount. He dropped low away from Mangas, and with his sharp riding-heeled boot came back with a hard kick and Mangas flew onto his back in the sand, his nose spurting blood. In almost the same motion the Don was back upright in the saddle, in the stirrups, giving his heels to his mount. He was fifty yards in the lead, bent low in the saddle, his hands still bound behind before Louie could get to his chestnut and get mounted. Enano was struggling to get back in the saddle and took off forty yards behind Louie.

Elizabeth was quickly on hands and knees behind Mangas, who was on his butt, facing away, both hands on his nose trying to stem the bleeding.

With surprising agility, exhausted as she was, she clambered to her feet, snatched up a rock the size of her head, and charged Mangas. He heard her coming and was turning as she smashed it atop his head. She didn't tarry to observe what damage she might have done, but ran to his horse, the closest one, gathered the reins, and with Mangas flat on his back, blood pooling from both his head and nose, gave heels to the red roan and spun back the way they'd come.

She screamed a rebel yell, unbecoming for a fine songbird, but encouraging for the horse, and the gelding leaped into a hard gallop.

Now if only the gelding, and she, could last, and if only the Don would lead the others on a long chase, she had a chance. She said a silent prayer he would escape, but doubted it. Even so superior a horseman as he might be, he had his wrists bound behind him.

She continued the silent prayer that she'd run into Stinman and a Prescott posse, if there really was one on their trail, and do so before the outlaws ran her down.

Settling into a ground-eating lope, she ignored her sore butt.

***

Hatch, rather sheepishly, stood beside Horace McCabe, surveying the damage the two groups of amateur lawmen had done to each other.

Two of Horace's posse had pounded the trail back toward Wickenburg, one was lying dead, bleeding out from a gutshot, Harry Higginbottom was shot through a forearm and, although they had stopped the bleeding, had a broken bone. They'd have to splint it before he could be expected to return even as far as Wickenburg. Both Horace and Hatch were unscathed, except for Hatch picking ocotillo spines from his right thigh and calf.

They'd had to make a fire and rest, letting the shivers reside. They made a pot of coffee and took their time, all of them absorbing the calamity of what had happened, saying little to each other.

"Maybe," Hatch finally said, "it's fittin' the fella what fired on us first is layin' dead there."

That got the hackles up on Horace's neck and he spoke through clenched teeth. "Lanny Quince has a new young wife at home, a wife swole up with child. If you assholes had announced yourselves, we'd be sharing information now rather than fixin' to drape him over his horse."

Hatch backed away a step and glared at Horace. "If memory serves, I did call out."

"Yep, you did. You said 'riders, drop your reins.' You

might have said 'I'm Marshal, whatever the hell your name is', and if so, my man might not have got nervous and snapped off that shot. He'd just heard of two shot dead not a half block from his little house, one of them his friend, the other his friendly grocer."

"Well," Hatch said, his tone a little milder, "what's done is done. Who was shot dead? In Wickenburg, I mean?"

"Our town marshal and the mercantile proprietor who never hurt a soul in his life, nor had Marshal Tommy Thompson except in his sworn duty…who happens to be my brother-in-law and has two beautiful daughters and a fine wife…my sister. *Was* my brother-in-law, I guess I should have said."

"Well," Hatch managed, "it's all water under the bridge now. Let's pack him up and we'll help get him back to Wickenburg. I need to get on the wire in case this pack of coyotes head out to Phoenix or other abodes and your town is the closest. Hells bells, they may have headed east from Wickenburg."

"Let's get it done," Horace said as Hatch turned and hoofed it back down the two-track to his horse. When he arrived, he was surprised to find his sorrel still, flat on his side in the trail, blowing blood from his nostrils. He bent to see a bullet wound in the animal's side and his yell could be clearly heard back up the trail where the others were loading Lanny across the saddle of his mount.

"God damn the blue belly flies and all that's holy!" Hatch yelled.

Then a pistol shot rang out as he put his animal out of its misery.

He followed that up with, "Hold up tying that man on his saddle. He's got to ride the rump. One of you bastards just killed the finest sorrel in Arizona Territory."

"Too bloody bad," Horace mumbled under his breath.

The sun was near overhead before they 'bit the proverbial bullet' and mounted up to ride back to Wickenburg and fess up to what had happened.

It was barely on the cool side of noon when they set out.

***

After a breakfast of Mrs. Fitzpatrick's jerky and cold biscuits, Rolondo and Skeeter had set a hard pace, loping a mile or two then walking a mile, depending upon the terrain. They'd been riding hard and were having trouble finding water. Rolondo was in the lead, and raised a hand indicating they stop. They reined up and he pointed at a pair of doves winging overhead.

He waved Skeeter up alongside, and in the low voice they'd taken to using, whispered, "Them mourning doves go to water twice a day. Let's hunker down here and see if'n we can figure them coming or going." Only moments later, they spotted another pair winging much lower and dropping into some scrub pine at the base of a basalt cliff only a hundred paces to the north.

"They could be nestin' up there," Rolondo said, then another pair settled in between the nearby pines.

"Worth a look?" Skeeter asked.

"Dang sure," Rolondo said, and they reined that way.

Sure enough, there was a trickle of a stream working its way out of the base of the cliff, ponding in a two-foot-deep, twenty-foot-round pool, then streaming out again for twenty feet before being absorbed into the soil.

They gave each other a grin as they slipped from the saddles, untying their water bags, loosening their cinches, and letting their animals wander in while they moved away and dropped to their stomachs and drank. They filled their bags.

"How far to where?" Skeeter asked.

"Still a fer piece. Cibola, and the ruins of Fort Wingate."

"Betwixt here and there…savages?"

"Only 'Pache, Zuni, and Navaho."

"Bad?"

Rolondo grinned with a shake of his head. "Them Mescalero will tear off your head and piss down your neck hole, but the Zuni and Navaho will just tear off'n your head."

"Comforting, thanks, friend. I guess we continue to ride quiet."

"As a squirrel hiding from a circling hawk," Rolondo said, with a laugh.

"How far to this Cibola?"

"Hundred miles. Lots of it in this pine country, so we won't get too damn cooked."

"We got time to strip down and soak the sweat off? Likely to be the last pond we see for a month of Sundays," Skeeter asked hopefully.

"I guess you didn't notice them tracks?"

"Hell, there's tracks ever'where."

"Yep, deer, elk, mountain sheep, but it's them unshod horse track you should be worried about. We ain't the only two legged critters usin' this water."

"Not surprised," Skeeter said, looking over his shoulder, then added, "Let's get the hell to poundin' trail."

"My figurin' exactly," Rolondo said, and they headed for their mounts.

They pulled up short, hearing something breaking brush, and whatever it was, it was coming their way.

Chapter Fifteen

***

Elizabeth would have been in Vulture City had Mangas's horse not stepped in a damn snake hole and busted his foreleg. She'd flown off as if launched from a medieval trebuchet. She felt as if gravel was embedded in her cheeks, and both her shoulder and back were badly bruised…she prayed not broken.

Dawn found her hunkered under the shade of a mesquite, trying to recover enough to get on her feet and use shank's mare to get to Vulture, or to run into a posse hunting the outlaws. As much as it also soured her stomach to remember the splatter of blood when she brought the stone down with all her strength, it cheered her somewhat to think she might have hit the one-eyed bandit hard enough to send him to Hell, as that would be one less outlaw on her trail.

She was sorry she hadn't collected herself in time to put the sorrel out of his misery, but by the time she sat up, she saw him three-legging it into the ocotillo, mesquite, and saguaro. It made her sick to think of the animal becoming fodder for the wolves or a cougar, then the buzzards.

And it made her sick that water skin was tied to the

saddle, departing with the horse. She thought of stumbling after him, but it was a fleeting thought. Even a three-legged horse could move more quickly through the desert spines than she could.

After two hours collecting herself, she managed to get to her feet. She was bruised badly, but didn't think anything was broken. At least not an ankle or leg, as she began to pick a foot up and put it in front of the other. By the time the sun was dead overhead and she had almost no shadow, she was struggling along, counting one hundred steps, then resting with hands on her knees. She rested for the slow count of twenty-five, then stumbled on.

As the desert warmed, she began to perspire until her garments were soaked, and had to keep wiping the sweat out of her eyes. She thought of leaving the wide well-traveled trail to pick a route through the cover of underbrush, as her pursuers would be coming behind her, but moving through the underbrush, even in this fairly flat terrain, was out of the question.

Besides, she should be able to hear a galloping or loping horse at enough distance to be able to move off and hide. The trail followed a winding arroyo, and there was plenty of underbrush to keep her hidden. And she would be able to hear hoofbeats.

With the sun directly overhead, even with the sunbonnet Louie had purchased for her, her lips began to chaff. In another hour, she couldn't make spit. She decided then and there that even Louie and a water bottle would be better than laying down to die in the heat.

Then she realized her hearing was occluded by a buzzing sound. Katydids, she wondered. She'd heard of the insects, and the buzzing was loud.

She winced with a pain in her left foot, moved to the side

of the trail, and sat on a boulder. It was a sharp pebble that had pierced the thin sole of her deerskin boots. She was able to dislodge it. She flung it over her shoulder, then clamped her teeth as the spine quivering buzz of the rattlesnake made her freeze, unmoving. The former thought of katydids was wishful thinking.

All she needed now, with every joint aching as if she'd been beaten for hours by a crazed Scotsman with a cudgel, with her lips beginning to split and her tongue seeming to swell, was a venomous snakebite.

Hell, she thought, *maybe ending it with a snakebite was better than dying in a scorching desert sun.*

Neither held much appeal.

She'd been saving the five shots in the revolver for a snake of another kind, when she was sure the shooting would set her free. But the thought of a snake sinking its fangs into her ankle was too much. The split-leather lady's riding skirt was much more difficult to manage than a loose one, but still she managed with the encouragement of the rattle

The buzzing stopped. She slowly looked over her shoulder to the rattler, moving only six or eight feet away in a crazy side looping motion. It was three feet or so in length, but the noise made it sound ten feet.

Her vision was not so good, but she cocked and fired, kicking up dust beneath the reptile, then fired and fired again, beside and beyond. Missing with four shots. But the snake, which had been moving perpendicular, now was, thank God, retreating.

She sunk to her rump on a rock, carefully centering her gaze on every stick or pattern that look like it could possibly be another snake. She hadn't cried in a score of years, and so was surprised when tears found their way down her dusty cheeks, leaving muddy tracks.

Leaping to her feet, she stumbled into the center of the trail, where she could see the ground for many feet around. She did not want to step on a rattlesnake. Or even see a snake of any kind.

Then she did.

Reined up a hundred feet behind her sat Louie, on his chestnut, a lazy grin on his face. He was snake enough, but strangely, at the moment, a thankful sight.

"Hey, Chiquita, little songbird, where are the Indians? Or were you shooting at ghosts? After a while in the desert, we all see ghosts."

"Snake," she managed, then managed to yell, "unless you want some of the same, ride away."

He laughed, and spurred his Morgan her way.

She raised the revolver and let him get no more than twenty paces, then, hoping one of the two wavering images of him was the right one, fired.

He'd leaned far out of the saddle, almost tumbling, but recovered as his chestnut did a side step with the report. Then he laughed again. "I know that nasty little pocket pistol, and it's a five-shot so you must reload before I get there and put you over my knee and enjoy tanning your behind."

"Go to hell," she managed, but slipped the revolver back in her skirt pocket.

He gigged the chestnut forward and dismounted, untying a goat-gut water bag. "I wouldn't be surprised if you want a little water?" A somewhat triumphant tone in his deep voice.

Without apology, Elizabeth croaked, "Yes. Now, please."

"Hand over the *pistola*, Songbird, and you'll have a

drink."

She did so, without comment.

Louie dismounted with a laugh and strode over and handed her the goat-gut water bag. "Just a little. More a little later."

She took two big gulps then felt as if she was going to throw up, and considered him right. Wise, not stingy. She poured a little in her hand and wiped her face, then the back of her neck. Tempted to pour it down her back, she restrained herself. Unladylike, and sure as Hades is hot, it could be water they'd be desperate for later.

"Now, Songbird," Louie said with an ironic tone, "now that you've enjoyed your little outing, it's time to get serious. We head for Puerto Peñasco."

"And Don Mateo?" Elizabeth asked.

"He's a little bruised, his ego mostly, and resting, enjoying Enano's company."

"And Mangas?" She silently hoped he was on his way to hell, because if not, he'd be awaiting the chance to send her wherever God had plans for her.

"He must have fallen off his horse. For a vaquero he was never much of a horseman. How he landed right on top of his *cabeza* on that hard rock, I'll never guess. We threw a few rocks over him so it will take the coyotes a while to feast on his ugly hide." Then he laughed as if she'd killed a rattler, not a man.

He grabbed her under an arm and swung her into the saddle behind him, on the sorrel's wide rump.

Twisting in the saddle so he could see her, he got serious. "If you reach for my *pistola* you'll find it's strapped well into its holster and it will make me very angry. You are fortunate you have yet to see me angry. Make me angry and you will not return to your family unsoiled. *Comprendes?*"

"If you don't mind, I will lay my head on your back and take a small nap."

"My pleasure, Songbird," he said, and gigged the chestnut into a lope.

***

Skeeter and Rolondo had ridden farther than they meant to. Having crested a small rise and seeing a tendril of smoke from a campfire in the distance, they rode within a quarter mile, before quickly retreating, upon seeing an Indian encampment. It caused them a long extra half mile up a brushy mountain, across a rock outcropping below a hundred-foot cliff, and a slippery shale descent that had Rolondo saying "sweet Jesus," a dozen or more times. The mule Skeeter rode was as steady as the rock cliff they rode below, but Rolondo's pinto was as skittish as a cuckolder hiding in the closet.

Finally, after returning to the bottom of the steep shouldered valley and the trail, which wasn't much more than a game thoroughfare, they came upon a grassy meadow. Moving off the trail fifty paces, they dismounted, watered the stock from the goat-gut water bag using the pitch covered nose bag, and pinned them with the picket pin through the reata. It gave both animals near twenty feet of wander room. Even if they pulled the pin, they'd tangle up in the near brush.

They kept a cold camp, encouraged by the sighting of the Indian camp.

As they rolled out their bedrolls, Skeeter couldn't help but ask, "Didn't you say you could palaver with the savage?"

"I did, and I can, but I'd surely prefer to know it's friendlies. I'd soon as have my curly locks from ear to ear across my noggin rather than on some brave's coup stick."

"What be a coup stick?"

That led to a half-hour palaver on the ways of the savage. Rolondo did not bother to go into the many ways the Apache and Yaqui enjoyed watching a white man die slowly. Figured it better Skeeter get a good night's sleep.

***

The kin had to ride hard toward the San Francisco peaks, believing a posse would be on their tail. They had no idea how many bodies they'd left face down in the dirt in Prescott when they'd sprung Ryan, but knew more than one. And they had a clear conscience that those they expired were the same who'd lied at trial and cost him three years in the Yuma hellhole.

Elizabeth's brother, Ryan O'Rourke, had been jailed and was due to be hanged as soon as the circuit judge showed up and they had a mock trial.

But his family, younger sister Kathleen, who went by her stage name Elizabeth Anne Graystone, and his cousins, Ethan and Dillon McCabe, Reece and Garret O'Connor, had come to his aid, busted him out and all were on their way home: Ethan and Dillon all the way to Montana where they ranched. Reece was headed to Leadville where he knew his talents with a Colt would fetch good earnings. Garret had hopes of finding work at his preferred trade, a teacher of literature, not that firearms were alien to him— he'd been a sharpshooter in service of the Confederacy.

The hell of it was all of them were family—kin—and kin meant more than just a little something to all of them.

It was life and death, if it came to that.

The fact was when they were all young, way too young to take advantage of their grandfather's fine sour mash whiskey, they'd taken a blood oath. Wrong one of the kin, and you'd wronged them all.

They'd carefully passed through Flagstaff, as it had had the wire as long as any Arizona town. The Beale Road passed through, all the way to California, and Reece and Garret both considered turning west for a new start, but both decided Leadville and Denver were their best opportunity, even though heading northeast would take them through Navajo and Hopi country. But with the four of them, they had confidence…maybe too much confidence.

Now the quest was to rescue Kathleen O'Rourke.

Chapter Sixteen

***

Reece had run into an old army chum, Trace Coo-
per, when they'd stopped at Whipple's Saloon in Flagstaff.
The town was still small, but growing and had the wire,
and they were particularly pleased to note that no sheriff
or marshal was partaking of Whipple's good whiskey.

They were a day's hard ride, over forty miles north
and nearing the Colorado River, when they'd camped,
and were surprised when Dillon, who had the first turn at
guard, awoke them all.

"What the hell," Reece groused, "it ain't midnight yet."

Garret corrected him, which he enjoyed doing,
"You mean it isn't midnight yet," and glancing up at
the moon, agreed, "but darn if you aren't right even if
barely intelligible."

"You can shove your 'intelligible' where the sun don't
shine," Reece continued to grouse.

Dillon snapped at them, "Knock it off. We're going back."

"You're nuts," Reece said.

Dillon handed him a paper, then motioned to a man
near the still glowing campfire. "Y'all met my old buddy

Trace. He rode straight through to catch up."

"What's this?" Reece questioned as he walked to where Trace was stirring up the fire to try and heat what was left in the coffee pot. He arrived at the flickering light and read. "Damn the flies, the Mexicans, the red devils, and every damn outlaw clawed his way out of his mama's womb."

"What?" Garret asked.

"Kathleen...Elizabeth has gone missing."

"Missing?" Garret asked again, "missing how?"

"This wire is from that deputy in Prescott, Josh, his name was."

Ryan, Elizabeth's brother, leaped off his bedroll and snatched the wire out of Reece's hand and read it. "Outlaws shot up the stage, stolt the box, grabbed her off twixt Prescott and Wickenburg. No one's heard of her three days hence."

Reece shook his head, and said with sarcasm, "Damn, if it was Ryan again, I'd say good riddance, but Kathleen? Heat the coffee, we'll ride out and gnaw some jerky and hardtack on the trail."

As Ryan rolled up his bedroll, he yelled over his shoulder. "Y'all done enough. Go on your way. I'll fetch my little sis back and send those who snatched her away straight to hell."

Garret stood with hands on hips. "Well, now aren't you the appreciative one? Shut your pie hole and pack up. She's your sis, but she's our cousin...and kin is kin."

Ryan stopped his packing and waved the kin together. "Look, you've all gone way out of your way to save my hide and I appreciate it. The rest of us are tumbling tumbleweeds, but," he eyed two of his cousins, "Ethan and Dillon have a ranch to run and those cattle they've worked so hard to build up will be spread all to hell and gone over

Montana they don't get back. You two go on. If the rest of us get our tit in a crack, we'll yell out. Reece, Garret and I can handle some worthless trash gone to robbing."

Reece and Garret both agreed, and finally Ethan and Dillon conceded, and the kin parted ways.

***

Skeeter and Rolondo heard brush busting and quickly gathered their mounts lead ropes and as quietly as possible, moved into the brush on the opposite side of the sounds.

In little more than a whisper, Rolondo said, "Ain't Indians as we'd never have heard them a'comin'."

"So, what?" Skeeter replied, slipping his new-to-him Winchester 66 from the saddle scabbard.

"Gonna know soon."

Almost as soon as he got it out, a big five by five mule deer buck, broke from the brush dragging a wolf on his hocks as another was lunging at his throat. Before Skeeter could collect himself and react, the second wolf succeeded in his throat attack and two others broke from the brush and one leaped atop the buck, which sunk to his fore-knees.

Rolondo fired his scattergun and blew one wolf back into the brush, and Skeeter gutshot another, and the three still on their feet—one badly wounded—scattered into the brush and were quickly gone.

The buck, his throat badly ripped, one hind leg dragging, tried to get away, but Skeeter broke his neck with another shot and dropped him in his tracks.

"Too much shootin'" Rolondo muttered.

"Too much meat to leave," Skeeter replied.

"Let's work quick, liver, heart, hindquarters and back strap, and let's pound trail."

Almost before he'd finished his suggestion, Skeeter was on the buck and in ten minutes they were working their way back to the trail and on their way to Cibola.

Rolondo yelled up to Skeeter, "Wish I'd had time to skin that wolf. Always wanted me a wolf pelt."

Skeeter laughed. "You blew that ol' wolf damn near in half. You'd had two pelt pieces."

"Maybe we'll see another pack on the trail."

"Them three that beat feet into the brush will be busy on the leavin' for a while. Two likely as one of 'em for sure died hard gutshot."

"Don't break my heart. I ain't fond of the buggers."

"Let's stay quiet. It's them other buggers I worry about and if any savages are in earshot, sure as Hell's hot, they be comin' to see what the shootin' is all about."

***

Louie and Elizabeth returned to where Mangas was now under a pile of rocks, and Enano sat in the shade. The pack string, Enano's pinto, and Elizabeth's newly acquired palomino grazed a patch of grass surrounded by a natural fence of cholla, the only escape blocked by Enano's reata.

Don Mateo was in the scant shade of a mesquite, on his belly, hogtied uncomfortably, trying to use his breath to blow ants away.

Enano saw them coming and recovered the palomino and led him out of the containment and to the pile of packs and saddles. He seemed irritated that there wasn't a rock he could mount to saddle her animal, but pulled its tack apart from the others and waited for Louie.

He also seemed irritated that her arms were wrapped around Louie's waist and her head rested on his shoulder as she dozed.

Louie reined up and gave Enano a tight smile. "Good job with the stock," he said.

But Enano's attentions were to Elizabeth as she lifted her head and glanced around.

"Hey, Songbird, what you do with Mangas's *caballo*?" Enano questioned. Then seeing Elizabeth's scraped and skinned cheekbone, turned accusingly to Louie. "You hit lady?"

"No, Sir Galahad, I did not. She took a dive off her mount."

Elizabeth stretched her arms and began a yawn, then flinched and let out a little mew as she was terribly sore. When she recovered, she eyed the little man and replied. "He stepped in a hole and, I'm sorry to say, broke a foreleg. He limped into the desert."

"With saddlebags?" Enano asked.

She nodded. "Saddlebags, saddle, bridle—"

"There was fine belly gun in those bags," Enano groused, as Louie saddled her palomino and saddled and hung packs on the packhorses and mules.

She walked over to Don Mateo. "Are you badly hurt?"

"I will heal," he said quietly. Then added, "I am sorry the scum caught up with you."

"There will be another day," she said with a low voice.

Louie yelled at them. "Stop your palaver. There will be no scheming."

"I'm going to untie him. He can't mount his horse bound as he is."

"Go ahead, but leave his wrists bound," Louie said, then cautioned, "Don Mateo, I will not stress my animal riding you down should you again give heels to your mount. I will merely shoot you between the shoulder blades and leave you for the buzzards. *Comprendes?*"

"I understand. I look forward to seeing the sea and feeling a cool breeze."

"Let me rein," Elizabeth called out to Louie.

"Swear on your sainted mama's grave you won't bolt, and you can rein," he replied over his shoulder.

"I swear." She said it, but wondered if her sainted mother would forgive her if she lied. Her ma was a survivor, and taught she and Ry to be the same.

Chapter Seventeen

***

Louie led the saddled animal over and helped her into the saddle, as she again let out an audible moan.

"I do believe," he said with a grin, "you will honor your oath. But, unfortunately, not because you enjoy our company. You will be pleased to learn we will layover a day outside Gila Bend to rest the horses and allow you a little time to heal. Then we face the sand and lava flows."

As they settled into the trail, and as it was wide enough, she reined up next to Louie.

"You called Enano 'Sir Galahad'. Are you a fan of the Knights of the Round Table?"

"And Shakespeare, and a few of the poets. I have a small library at Puerto Peñasco you might enjoy while we await your ransom."

"Which poets?" Elizabeth asked. Maybe there was a little more to this Welshman than she'd thought.

"Dickenson, Lord Byron, Robert Burns, and my favorite," and he began reciting,

"It was many and many a year ago,

In a kingdom by the sea,
That a maiden there lived whom you may know
By the name of Annabel Lee;
And this maiden she lived with no other thought
Than to love and be loved by me.

I was a child and *she* was a child,
In this kingdom by the sea,
But we loved with a love that was more than love—
I and my Annabel Lee—
With a love that the wingèd seraphs of Heaven
Coveted her and me."

"Poe. Can you recite others?" Elizabeth asked.

"A few, and that one to all the way to its melancholy end:

In her sepulcher there by the sea—
In her tomb by the sounding sea."

She stared at him for a moment, he gave her a wink and she quickly looked away. Then she mumbled, "I shouldn't say so, but I'm surprised and impressed."

"Aw, Songbird," he said, with unblinking eyes that seemed to darken even more, "I have many talents and will surprise you more when you have succumbed to my charms. I am, after all, a romantic Welshman."

"Ha," Elizabeth said with a bit of a snarl, purposely seeming more exasperated than she actually was. He was a charming lout, in a horrid sort of way. She shook her head violently as if trying to expel the thought, then almost passed out from the pain. He was a murdering scoundrel, and it was his fault she was in this miserable condition, that she must remember.

"Where are we going? A place with a bath, I hope," she asked as they clomped along.

"You ain't dropping no bread crumbs, are ya?" he challenged.

She laughed. "Sure, from that wonderful French croissant I had for breakfast. Even if I did the birds and lizards would gobble them up before they could lead my white knights to save me."

"Lizards don't eat nothin' but flies and such."

She was silent a moment, then asked, "Why don't you use the proper king's English. Obviously you are an educated man."

"Bugger the king."

"And why are you profane? You know it doesn't become an educated man."

"Bugger education. I sought it but the bloody English only accepted those they deemed upper crust. So, bugger the English too. Present company excepted." Then he looked off at a setting sun that quivered like a blob of molten brass on a sheet of flat iron. "Then again, maybe not." Then he guffawed.

She ignored him for a while as the sun set and the sky turned vermillion, then repeated her question, "Please don't be rude. Now, a place with a bath, I hope?"

"I told you. I'm surprised you don't believe me. Tomorrow we'll come on the Gila River, a pretty impressive canyon in places. Late tomorrow we'll start into the real red rock country, the next day we'll wander into Gila Bend, the town so named as the river makes a ninety-degree turn west toward the Colorado and Yuma. Was only a stage station, but now they got a real town, and a hotel with a bath shed out back and a bathhouse on the edge of town. Hot water 'til you shrivel up like a prune. That's the good of it. The bad is they got the wire and are liable to be lying in wait for the likes of us. And if I can't trust a songbird not to sing out about who we might be, then I'd have to go to shooting some poor dumb pilgrims."

"I don't want anyone killed. I'll ride in with you, have my bath, and ride back out...and I swear on my sainted mother's grave I'll stay mum."

"Done, but of course I'll have to get in that bath with you just to make sure you keep your word."

"Same chance as the sun that's just disappearing turning around and coming back up."

He laughed and slapped his thighs. "The Chinaman who runs the bathhouse only has one door on the place. You swear and I'll grab up some hooch and park my own self outside that door a sip away while you get the road dust outta all your pretty cracks and crevices."

"A deal, and again, your rudeness doesn't become you."

"And, by the way," he said, his voice turning deep, "if'n you should run into the arms of the law while in Gila Bend and there were too many for me to gut and filet, then Don Mateo will die hard before we ride out for the sand and lava country."

"He's a gentleman, and you should take a lesson," her eyes flashed at him like a cougar eyeing a tender fawn. "That said, I wouldn't risk harm to him."

"Then we got us a deal."

***

Rolando and Skeeter had traded their pack ani-mals plus a little gold coin for sound riding stock in Flagstaff and now rode good animals and dragged a second solid mount. They could make seventy or eighty miles a day, country permitting, switching from one to the other, and they'd likely give out before the stock. Three of the four saddlebags each man carried on two of the mounts were filled with rolled oats, the fourth with personal folderol and spare ammo. They carried only one set of saddlebags on the mount they forked as they'd let the second animal carry as little as possible, only a set of saddlebags rim full of oats and personals, rigged with a latigo. Fuel for the ride ahead of them.

Fort Verde lay halfway to Prescott where two stage roads merged, the one heading nearly due south from Flagstaff and the other heading southwest from Cibola and Jerome. As the trails merged, so did a pair of riders on the Cibola and three from Flagstaff, all at a lope. And all pulled up, eyeing each other for a moment before Rolando spoke up.

Both he and Skeeter had hands resting on the butts of their sidearms, as did the three rough-looking horsebackers facing them.

And both groups had animals with heaving sides and withers dripping foam.

It was obvious both were running after…or from something or someone.

Chapter Eighteen

***

"Y'all running from savages?" Rolando yelled as the lathered horses from both groups blew and caught their wind.

Ry gigged his gray and the sorrel he was dragging closer, no reason to yell. "We ain't seen hide nor hair of any. You?"

"Way behind us, but we skirted them. Where y'all headed…maybe we could ride together…more likely to keep our hair?"

"We aren't going into the fort. We're headed south of Prescott, at least all the way to Wickenberg…maybe Mexico."

"I'll be stoppin' in Prescott, but my friend Skeeter here is likely headed on. What's your business?"

Ry ignored the question but nudged his mount even closer, eyeing the huge black man on the thick necked mule.

"Skeeter?"

"That's what I'm called."

"John Axe…that Skeeter?"

"Who's askin'?" Skeeter said, a little suspiciously.

"Elizabeth Anne Graystone's brother, Kathleen O'Rourke's brother, if you know her by that name. She's spoken of you with respect. She said you were hopefully on the mend all the way up in Pueblo."

"Don't know nothing about no Kathleen O'Rourke, but I'm in the employee of Miss Graystone. And I'm riding to fetch her from some no-goods."

"Damned," Ry said, with a tight smile as he dismounted, "if there ain't a God in heaven moving us all about like chess pieces. Our quest is the same."

He moved close and extended a hand, which was lost in Skeeter's big paw. Skeeter gave him a grin and a nod in agreement.

As the sun was a quarter high over the eastern horizon behind lace clouds, Reece, Garret and Ryan, and their two new associates, skirted Fort Whipple, the Headquarters of the Military Department of Arizona and home of the 10th Calvary Regiment, known to many as the Buffalo Soldiers. Even though the military was busy with the Indian Wars and seldom involved themselves with domestic law matters, Ry had no interest in running into a troop who might ask questions.

The good news was neither the kin nor Skeeter and Rolando had need of the black boys in blue during their sojourn up to the Colorado River and back. No sign of the savage.

"Daren't we wander in for some hot breakfast?" Garret questioned.

"Sure as that sun is arising we'll run into a law dog or one of the other louts who'll recognize me...odds are there's posters on every other ponderosa by now, and we'll have to fight our way out."

Reece was adamant. "We've seen enough of Prescott. Skirt it on the north and grain the horses and grub up at

Iron Springs, then head out for Wickenberg. We'll get more than halfway there before the stock gets too weary to push. Even us switching off mounts time to time."

As they left the trail to skirt Prescott, Rolando called out, "I got kin here and will be leaving y'all."

Reece rode between Rolando and Skeeter as they were saying their goodbyes. He eyed Rolando, and it was less than a friendly stare. "We got reason to fight shy of Prescott, and you'd be well advised not to mention you saw us on the trail nor where we're headed."

"Well, sir, I got no reason to flap my jaw about y'all. Besides, your new friends of mine, I hope, and sure enough of Skeeters...so my lips are done sealed like I been a'lappin' horse hoof glue."

"Not even if a wanted poster offered you a barrel full of coin?"

"Ain't enough coin in the territory for me to cause a dollop of trouble for Skeeter."

"Ain't Skeeter I'm worried about."

"Trouble for y'all would likely be trouble for Skeeter. Black man riding with a wanted man would likely be hung right alongside. Seems that's one place we's all equal."

Ry had to smile at that. "Well, sir, you got a point. Just so you know, you cause one of us trouble, you cause all of us trouble, and those who cause the kin trouble most often end up in a bad way."

"You got my word, sir."

"And your word is good with me." He extended a hand and shook with Rolando. "And one more thing," he flipped a ten-dollar gold piece to Rolando. "Give five of this to Deputy Josh Clemmons. Tell him you ran into Miss Elizabeth Anne Graystone's kin way back up the trail somewhere. That's for his kindness sending a wire to Flagstaff. That should be a dollar for the wire and four dollars for a steak and bottle of good hooch for him and his lady, a tip, and a pair of tickets to the theater. And you keep the other five for your trouble."

"Yes, sir. Deputy Josh. And I keep five? Mighty generous of you, sir."

It was near noon when they made Iron Springs, watered, grained, and tied their animals at a rail out back, out of the way of any coach and six up that might wander in, and entered to eat.

The lady of the station eyed them all carefully, then advised, "We don't serve negros or Indians inside. Should your man want to go on out—"

Ry interrupted her. "He's a free man, and not our man, ma'am. And we got plenty of jerky and hardtack in our saddlebags you don't want our business?"

"I didn't say that."

"I could advise the troops back at the fort that Buffalo soldier, negro, business isn't welcome and you'd just as soon not have them come to your aid should the Apache drop by for a bowl?"

"I didn't say that."

"No, ma'am. You said my friend wasn't welcome so I assumed—"

"You assumed wrong."

"Sign says two bits for a bowl and bread, and I got a silver dollar and dime tip says we all sit around that table. In fact, I got a silver dollar and four bits as my friend here will have two bowls."

She sighed deeply. "Let's get y'all fed and on down the road afore others arrive."

Ry just shook his head disgustedly.

"Obliged," Skeeter said just loud enough for Ry to hear.

They were spooning down the last of the generous bowls of Mrs. Stanford's venison and bean slumgullion with fist sized chunks of hard bread for soppin' when they heard riders rein up outside.

"You expecting anyone?" Ry asked the rail-thin station master's wife.

"Near lunchtime. I normally get a couple of hungry drovers or miners from the places here about. I'd hoped y'all would be on down the trail…."

Ry rose and carried his bowl to the lady, "The food was larrupin' good, ma'am," he said, then added, "but the welcome left some to be desired," but his eyes were on the door and he headed that way. Just as he reached it, it was flung aside, and he and Sheriff Hatch Stinman stood only six feet apart, both equally surprised, both with hands on the butts of their sidearms.

"You don't jerk that iron and I won't," Ry said with a low growl.

Chapter Nineteen

***

"How far to this Bend place?" Elizabeth asked as
they tightened the cinches after taking a short noon break."

"*Mañana*, midmorning, after we roost for the dark time.
You'll see the welcome sign of salt cedars, a mile wide at
places, a nice green sight…that presuming we don't get in
the way of Apache or Yaqui."

"What's special between here and there?"

"Them savages or *banditos* are fond of green just
like us."

"Sure, but why here, why Apache, Yaqui, or *banditos*,
why now?"

"From here on it's truly their country. We *gringos* been
late to the show. 'Cept near Gila Bend. Of course when I
say their country, I mean one month the Apache rules, the
next the Yaqui, then if the Mex is across the border and
platoon strength, they might have a say. I'd suggest you
stay tucked in close to Enano and ol' Louie."

"Enano?"

"Yep, you don't think I keep him around for his rough
and tumble fisticuff ability?"

"No, but he seems to carry his weight…such as it is."

"Yeah, but he don't tip the scale as much as a goat. Ain't his work ethic either," Louie laughed. "Them crazy redskins think he's some kind of special. Him being less than four feet tall. 'Bout three feet eight inches last we measured. Seems the savage thinks him a kind of god or some such. There's a whole passel of drawings on the cliffs down by the Gila and it's some runt like him lording over a tribe, killing pictures with this runt slaying horned critters. Hell, Enano is worth his weight in gold as he can jabber their lingo, both Apache and Yaqui, and what he can't say through them little brown teeth he can sign. I've never seen the like…"

She eyed him skeptically for a few moments, then decided he was telling the truth.

"So, what's our play should the Apache or Yaqui get between us and Gila Bend?"

"'Spose I could trade you for passage," he said, and laughed again.

"They'd likely be better company," Elizabeth replied. "I'm serious. What do we do?"

"You got lots of pretty things in that valise of yours. I got a couple of bottles of Who Hit John. Comes to it, we got extra firearms. Hell, we get in real trouble I'm sure they'd love that valise."

Elizabeth gritted her teeth. Her jewels and particularly the broach her mother gave her were hidden in the false bottom of her valise, so that wasn't an option unless they were about ready to stake her over an anthill.

"Mr. Bowen, I've tolerated a lot of insults from you. But if you let my lace things get away, you'll never hear me speak again."

"Nor sing?" he said, with a wide grin.

"Nor sing a B flat."

"How about you dress up in some of those lace things and let me decide. One of those red ones might be nice. I'll send Enano off to kill us a rabbit for supper."

"Mr. Bowen, not that it's any of your affair, but that's a corset cover, and there are corset and silk stockings and embroidered garters to match, all the way from Paris, France…but you'll not see so much as an ankle of mine, and surely no undergarments. Now, keep your eyes open for savages and you and I may continue to get along… such as it is." She reined back and fell in behind him and the mule he now led, and ahead of Enano who led Don Mateo, still with hands bound behind, and a leg over the lead rope of the two following packhorses.

Louie yelled back over his shoulder. "Woman, you hexed us." And he pointed. In the distance, a cloud of dust billowed above the saguaro and cholla. "Doubt if that's a marchin' band come to play for you to sing."

"I go see," Enano said, and reined up beside her and handed her the lead rope to Don Mateo's mount and the trailing horses and mule.

Enano galloped ahead and was soon out of sight.

"Aren't we going to hide?" Elizabeth called up to Louie.

"Wouldn't matter," Louie said over his shoulder. "Damn Apache can smell us from a half mile and the Yaqui likely a mile. Just sit tight until Enano returns."

Don Mateo spoke up, "You wouldn't leave me bound with the Yaqui near? The Yaqui have long wished to get their spears into a Santiago…any Santiago."

"Yes," Louie said, with a sardonic grin. "I heard tell you had a hundred vaqueros ride down on a Yaqui village and kill all…women, children, and all but a few who skedaddled."

"They were on Tejon Grande."

Louie turned to Elizabeth. "Your *haciendado gentile* has a little land grant of a hundred thousand acres or more. Yaqui land for many centuries before his papa showed up with a division of *soldados* during the border troubles. He was a tough old bird and gave Zach Taylor some fits so the *presidente* grabbed a land grant from the Zacaria family and gave it and another fifty thousand acres to papa."

But Elizabeth was stuck on the killing of women and children. "Don Mateo, you certainly didn't condone the killing of children?"

"*Señorita*, when men are in the fierce heat of battle, particularly against those who have killed many of their own, women and children among them, they…they are capable of things we do not want to speak of or have haunt our dreams. I was not there."

"That's something, I guess," she said, but wondered if he was being truthful. But they had more to worry about at the moment.

Don Mateo repeated his complaint. "You would keep me bound?"

Louie seemed to chew on it a moment, then dismounted and walked to a pack animal and removed some hemp line. He cut four feet from it and moved beside Don Mateo's mount. "I'm tying a noseband down to the martingale. You give heels to him and he'll try to run, but can't get his head up, and either face plant the both of y'all or go to hoppin' like one of them goofy kangaroos I saw at the Perkin's and Goodell Traveling Circus. He goes to hopping it'll make a hard shot for me to put one between your bony shoulder blades, but greaser, know I can do it."

"So, I'm to fight with my hands?"

Louie laughed. "I guess you can dismount and go to running, but them Yaqui can run a hundred miles in this desert, even dismounted. I saw some nice tuna cactus back aways. You can slap 'em with a paddle. But leastways you won't be bound up."

"I accept that," Don Mateo said, almost appreciatively.

Almost as Louie finished untying Don Mateo's wrists, they heard the pounding of hooves. Enano slid his lathered mount to a dust billowing stop, caught his breath, then gasped, "Yaqui, two dozen, no women, no *muchachos*."

Then he looked back over his shoulder, as twenty Yaqui braves lined up along a low rise, all with animals aimed their way.

Chapter Twenty

***

Sheriff Hatch Stinman carefully removed his hand from the butt of his revolver, but didn't back away. He knew Ryan O'Rourke from long experience, had no advantage, and no surety he could outdraw his former friend. In fact, he was sure he couldn't.

"I got two men backin' me up, Ry. So why don't you just hand it over and come along peaceful like?"

"Your two don't trump my three, Hatch. And two of them have a real bone to pick with you."

"What bone?"

Ry had no interest in letting Hatch and the people of Prescott know that Elizabeth Anne Graystone was really Kathleen O'Rourke and his sister, as it would implicate her in his barely-a-week-old escape from the Prescott jail and shootout with a number of Prescott's townsfolk, but he hoped if he'd sent any to their maker, they were those who'd wronged him and lied to get him thrown in that hellhole, Yuma Prison.

So, he lied. "My friends here heard you'd let their cousin get squired away by some outlaws. If she was your kin, would you think kindly of that?"

"Hell, I was in town and they—"

"They kidnapped her and killed a bunch of fellas."

"And killed the city marshal of Wickenburg and are likely killing poor folks in Mexico by now. We chased them halfway there—"

"Why not all the way?" Ryan challenged.

"We had some trouble—"

"Well, Hatch, you obviously couldn't handle that trouble and I damn sure guarantee you can't stand this trouble, so a wise man would tip his hat and ride on into Prescott and put his feet up on that desk and sip some good whiskey, whilst her kin and I, and her employee, go fetch her."

"You think you can outshoot the three of us? I don't see these other three you're blabberin' about." He was straining over his shoulder to see inside.

Reece stepped out from a far corner of the stage station. "Got tired of sittin', marshal." He carried a scattergun, muzzle trained on Rory Maxwell, still mounted and the closest to him.

Garret stepped forward around the other corner. "I had to get up afore finishing my pie, and that makes me downright crotchety and wanting to spill some blood." His Winchester was cocked and trained on Harry Higginbottom.

Neither of the mounted men that remained of Hatch's posse had seen what was coming, and, even though they were hard men who'd been vigilantes at one time or another, were caught flat-footed.

"Damn," Ry said, "if they aren't a sneaky lot. The only thing those two are better at than sneakin' is shootin'." Then he yelled at the two riders. "Fellas, I remember you from Prescott and have no grudge with you and don't have time to plant you, so two-finger your revolvers and stuff them in those saddlebags."

Ryan reached out and pulled Hatch's revolver. "I'll tuck this one away for you."

Before he could finish the sentence, Skeeter stepped up behind Ryan, reached out and spun Hatch around, grabbed him by the belt on either side of his waist, and picked him two feet off the ground and, with Hatch kicking and cursing, carried him to his mount and flopped him aboard.

"Who the hell—" Hatch started to complain.

Ryan laughed. Even he was surprised at Skeeter's actions, but managed to interrupt Hatch. "That would be Goliath. You heard of him? I guess the Good Book was wrong and David missed that sling shot."

Ryan followed them and shoved Hatch's revolver in his saddlebag. Then he said in a low but steady voice, "Now, Hatch, you were outnumbered and we had the drop on y'all, so there's nothing to be frettin' about here. Just ride on back and we'll continue to track the outlaws. I'd ask you to deputize me and the boys, but that might be asking a mite much. All that said, you got any pointers for us?"

Hatch hesitated, then finally complied. "All what I've heard, Louie, Llywelyn Bowen, is the stud-duck of that outfit, and he's been known to lay low in both Puerto Peñasco and Hermosillo. They didn't stock up at Wickenburg or Vulture, far as we could ascertain, so it's likely Gila Bend… if they stock up at all. And only a damn fool would try them lava flats without sustenance for man and beast."

"Obliged, Hatch. Don't bother rounding up another posse. We'll be moving hard and fast."

"Not faster than the wire," Hatch couldn't help but throw in.

"Nope, not faster than the wire. But you'd be putting a

bunch of city folk up against some hardened gun fighters," then he turned to Reece. "Hey, gunfighter, that white rock across the road?"

Almost as soon as he got it out, Reece had drawn and fired his Colt. Chips flew from the head sized rock, fifty feet away.

Ryan laughed. "And he's the slowest of the lot of us. And Goliath here can pick up his horse and throw it at you."

"Shut up, Ryan," Hatch groused. "We're gonna ride on into town and get some rest before deciding on what to do about you hooligans."

"Go with God, Hatch. I hope you live a long, prosperous, and happy bunch of years."

The three of them reined away, gave heels to their mounts, and galloped toward Prescott. Without reaching into their saddlebags.

Ryan yelled at the others. "Mount up. I want to make another twenty-five or thirty miles before we sack out."

As Reece mounted, he complained, "And I sure as hell ain't as slow as you louts."

Ryan yelled over his shoulder, "Remember what Stonewall said, 'Always mystify, mislead, and confuse the enemy.'"

"So?"

"So, if they think Ret and I are the fastest, they'll draw down on us first while you're ventilating their hides."

"Okay," he said, seeming satisfied. "If it comes to that, I'm happy with you two being first on the target list. Hell, I may even slow down a mite."

***

They'd stayed quiet, careful not to raise any dust, and the Yaqui band had ridden to a rise not a hundred yards away. The Indians stilled their animals and stared for several long moments, then seemed to chatter among themselves.

To Elizabeth's great surprise, Enano reined another twenty-five yards closer, then stood in the saddle, then to her shock switched ends and stood on his hands in the saddle. And she was more shocked yet when he flipped back to his feet, again standing.

As soon as he dropped back into the seat, the Indians reined away and dropped out of sight.

He gigged his horse back to recover the reins to the packhorses and mules from Elizabeth, and gave her a wide, brown-toothed grin. "Enano pretty good, eh, Miss Lady?"

She returned his grin with a smile, but quickly glanced back at the ridge, expecting the two dozen sinewy savages to come galloping over the rise, screaming and shooting, howling and firing rifles and arrows. They didn't. So, she added. "More than pretty good, my man. More, more, more than pretty good."

That elicited another broad grin, then they moved on.

They stopped to make a dry camp, but not until all hint of evening light was gone. Elizabeth was bone weary, still dehydrated, and her skin felt like lizard scales.

Louie walked over and handed her a gob of bacon grease. "This might help."

She gave him a tight smile and accepted his offering.

As she unrolled her bedroll near the fire, Enano pulled a tinder box from his saddlebag and quickly made a small cooking fire from cactus husks and dead mesquite. Louie sat down beside her.

"I been cogitatin', why'd you not use that little pea shooter before the snake came along…except, of course, when you shot my Mex friend twixt his beady eyes?"

"What makes you think I shot him?"

"I didn't think much about it until you went to shootin' at that snake and proved you had a weapon hid out."

"I saw no reason to shoot you dead, or Enano. But Mangas was another story. Luckily he fell on that rock—"

"Oh, you bet, that was lucky that his head ran into that rock you was holding—"

"Like I said, fell on that rock. You've been a gentleman, such as it is and more than might be expected, as had Enano. Had it come to it, make no mistake, I would have used it on either of you to make my escape."

"So, Songbird, how many of those little pea shooters or blades do you have hidden under those soiled garments of yours? Maybe it's time to find a water hole and strip you down to discover your hidden arms...or charms."

"And should you do so, I'd hate to see your head crushed by another rock you might fall upon."

He laughed and slapped his thighs. "So, Songbird, you swear upon your sainted mother's grave, for what that's worth...not her grave, your oath...that you have no blades or firearms hidden between those swollen breasts or silky thighs?"

"Does your language have no bounds, sir?"

"Please, Songbird, assure me."

"I have no blades nor firearms." She didn't mention the six-inch hatpin that secured the sunbonnet he'd given her. She supposed these rough men had never seen the damage the sharp pin could do. He merely nodded, then moved away to unroll his bedroll in the darkness away from the fire. He spoke over his shoulder.

"Sleep well. Tomorrow, Gila Bend, and if no badge interferes, or we don't get our hair lifted twixt here and yonder, you'll have that bath."

And so she dreamed of soaking in a hot tub. She also dreamed of the cold eyes of Yaqui savages staring at their camp from the undergrowth.

Chapter Twenty-One

***

The four following Louie Bowen and their kin moved with determination.

It was easier traveling with four rather than three as they would only spend six hours sleeping. At the day's end, one man would clean up and take care of the stock while the others snored, then he'd wake his replacement and would get to sleep while the others readied for the sixteen to eighteen hours of grind ahead. It also meant two-hour breaks to give each animal a couple of mouthfuls of grain and enough water to keep them going. A quick rub down and change of saddle and off they went alternating quick walk and lope, depending upon the country.

Half a day south of Vulture, where they'd resupplied with bacon, beans, a bottle of Black Widow whiskey, hardtack for the men, and refilled the rolled-oat saddlebags for the horses, they came upon a bunch-grass flat, cut by a three-foot-wide sweet water stream. They loosed the cinches and let the animals graze to save on their meager oat supply.

Ryan had spent two years busting caliche limestone and granite in Yuma Prison, then crossed the Sonoran

Desert to settle some grudges in Prescott, so he was more knowledgeable about surviving the changing landscape than his cousins or Skeeter.

As they lay in the sparse shade of a smoke tree, Ryan broke the restful silence, "If he's heading for Puerto Peñasco then Gila Bend has to be thirty or forty miles out of the way. Why go there?"

Garret lifted his hat off his face. "Nobody saw hide nor hair of them in Vulture, so if they didn't stock up there then it's likely they need more grub and grain. That marshal we ran into looked like a whipped dog, so this Louie likely thinks he's free of hounds sniffin' his trail. He's got a few pounds of gold and a wad of paper money. As I recall from talking about the country while we were waiting to spring you from that Prescott gray-stone hotel. Gila Bend ain't much, but ain't-much towns all got saloons, hot meals, cool beer, and maybe even a copper or leather bathtub and a Chinee girl to scrub your back. My bet is Gila Bend. Besides, he may be headed for the big town of Hermosillo. There ain't nowhere to crow about your newfound riches in Puerto Peñasco."

Ryan chewed on that a moment, then replied, "Yeah, but Hermosillo is all of a hundred miles more travel. And, God willing, he's still dragging sis along, and as y'all know, she can make life pretty damn miserable if she sets her mind to it. And the way to Hermosillo is through or near the rancho that Don Mateo is said to own. Maybe Bowen wants to get near that place to send in a demand for ransom but the Don likely has a hundred vaqueros licking their chops for what they'd be rewarded should they rescue their *Jefe*. I don't know about you, but I'd fight shy of being anywhere near a bunch of angry vaqueros who can likely ride to Denver without stoppin' for a single pee break."

Ret eyed him carefully. "How the hell do you know all

that…about this Don Mateo I mean?"

Ry shrugged his shoulders. "Lots of talk about him when I was in Prescott, and Trace had recent come to Flagstaff from Prescott and had all the scuttlebutt on the robbery."

Reece, always the skeptic, pulled his hat off his face. "This may be a damn fool's errand. Hell of it is, they may have headed for Phoenix and on into New Mexico, or even Texas. I'm already saddle sore and that hot copper tub in Gila Bend sounds good to me. I'd like some proof we're on the trail and that my pretty little cuz don't have this Louie fella carrying her bags and doing her calling."

Ryan could feel the heat rise in his backbone. "Reece, I don't think I can outdraw you, but if you don't want a crease, Reece, in your head bone from one of my hard fists you won't be doubting Kathleen."

"You think you're a poet? Garret's the literary type. And it's Elizabeth, remember."

Garret spoke up, "Both of you shut up and get a few minutes of rest. I vote Gila Bend. If he's holding both Kathleen…Elizabeth…and this Don Mateo for ransom, he'll be heading for Mexico to dodge the territory law, vaqueros or no vaqueros. And that settles it."

Ryan calmed down. "Gila Bend it is."

***

Elizabeth had been happy to awaken to a cool desert morning still in possession of her hair. Elano had, to her surprise, six desert quail turning over the fire. He'd set a box trap made of twigs, baited with seeds he'd harvested, with a trench lined with backward facing stiff grass. The quail followed the seed trail in and couldn't get out against the stiff grass.

Roast quail and coffee made for a fine breakfast. Sadly, they were in a dry camp again and she couldn't even do a facsimile of bathing, but with luck, if Louie could be believed, they'd be in Gila Bend in the afternoon. And there'd be a bath, thank God, a hot bath.

They rode without stopping for a break until they topped the canyon with the Gila River flat far below. Edging the river on both the north and south sides were thick salt cedars. In places, the thicket was a half mile wide. Some enterprising citizens, probably the express company owners, had invested a lot of time and money to cut a two-track road to the bottom through the red rock. There would be no passing, but it was wide enough for a coach. Gila Bend was fast becoming known as a crossroads of the southern Arizona Territory. With Prescott, the Territorial Capitol to the north, the growing city of Phoenix fifty miles to the northeast, Tucson to the east, Casa Grande to the southeast, Mexico fifty miles south, and Yuma, the gateway to California, to the west, it was an enviable location for freighters and travelers. For centuries the pueblo had been crossed by Hohokum, Pima, Apache and Yaqui Indians, and as early as 1670 by Spanish conquistadors and missionaries, and finally in 1865 by white men.

Luckily, they did not come head-to-head with a wide Conestoga express coach coming up as they descended. There was no getting lost in the salt cedars as they were thick as hair on a hog's back but the road had been widened in many places so coaches could easily pass. When they reached the riverside, there were clearings from high water killing the trees. On both sides of the trail, you could see blackened stone fire-rings where folks had made camp.

Louie spun his big Morgan around and stopped next to Enano, but before he could speak up, Enano snapped at him, "Your turn watch this *bastardo rico*. My turn ride to town."

Louie gave him a condescending smile. "Hey, little

amigo, I'm trusting you with the *haciendado*, worth *mucho dinero* to us, and with most the loot. How much more trust could any man put in an *amigo*?"

"That does not get me a hot meal not cooked myself, or hot *señorita*. Unless you want leave the songbird for my use——"

Elizabeth feigned shock. "Enano, I'm surprised at you! And you've been such a gentleman."

"I sorry, Miss Lady. But Mr. Louie been stingy gut long enough. I save my *amor* for town ladies——"

Louie guffawed, slapping his thighs. "Hey, *poquito*, *su amigo* Louie will return after he has discovered it safe for you. You must admit, you are more recognizable than a camel or an elephant. Your exploits and size are known all across the Sonoran. I, on the other hand, am a plain looking horsebacker riding with his *señora*. When we return, we will guard the Don and our winnings and you can settle between the *gordo* thighs of a *señorita*."

"Bowen," Elizabeth snapped, "you are a pig and your talk is akin to snorting and rooting. And winnings? You call the hard earned wages of many folks your winnings?"

Louie snorted twice, mimicking a rooting hog. Then laughed. "Call it what you will, Songbird, it's now ours. Which brings me to the subject of taking you among a good many pilgrims. Do you wish for that hot bath?"

"Of course."

"Then we can ride among the townsfolk without you causing them to lose their blood in the street or on the boardwalk by calling out?"

"I don't want to see any innocents killed on my account."

"And even if you change your mind, remember I have plenty of .44/.40s in my spinner and my Winchester, and I may have time to put one in your pretty backside should you disappoint me."

"Fine, but you remember I didn't put a little chunk of lead in your backside when I had the chance."

"Aww, Songbird, I sort of believe that was only because your aim was not so good and you didn't have exactly the right time to do so. But that is neither here nor there. Today is today and today is the time for you to choose, scatter the streets of Gila Bend with bloody townsfolk or enjoy a hot bath and maybe some sweet breads from the bakery. A Swiss couple has a fine establishment there, if they have remained in business."

Elizabeth turned to the little man. "Enano, would you please stay and guard the Don and what Louie calls your winnings so I can enjoy a hot bath?"

"I your servant, Miss Lady, but still not fair."

Louie doffed his hat and made a short bow to Enano. "The rose looks fair, but fairer we it deem for that sweet odor which doth in it live."

"What does that mean?" Enano asked, with a sour look.

Elizabeth answered. "It's out of a Shakespeare sonnet, Enano. It sort of means I'll be prettier if I don't smell like the mule."

"You smell pretty to me, Miss Lady."

"But I'll smell like a lilac, if you'll be so kind as to stay and let us go?"

Enano slipped out of the saddle and stomped away, leading Don Mateo's mount and the two horses and mule, tied as a string. He yelled over his shoulder at Louie. "Bring me bottle tequila or pulque, *amigo*," but the '*amigo*' was said with great sarcasm.

Louie waved at her, "Let's go, little songbird. Remember, only four miles and it's a hot bath or a blood bath, your choice."

Chapter Twenty-Two

***

Ryan, Reece, Garret and Skeeter left the grass flat fairly well rested and full of jerky and hardtack, and each had had a draw on a jug and their fill of water from a trickle they came upon before entering jagged ravine country that was thick with saguaro, cholla, violet prickly pear, and golden hedgehog cactus. It slowed them down for a couple of hours before they broke into dry and relatively open country.

Ry reined up. He waited until they'd all gathered up. He spoke directly to Skeeter. "Hey, big man. I'm not talking down to you, but you and that big Percheron mule are not accustomed to hard riding. I've no doubt you'll get anywhere we need to go, just that you'll not get there as fast as the rest of us. And you don't have a second mount like us'n." He turned to his cousins. "I think we got a chance to catch up if we risk killing a mount or two. We set a lope-gallop pace here on to Gila Bend. Agree?"

Reece and Garret both nodded.

Ry turned back to Skeeter. "You find your way to Gila Bend?"

"You likely gonna leave a trail like a herd of dem buffalo, so if'n I can't it's 'cause I done went blind."

Ryan laughed. "If'n you get lost, next river you come to is the Gila, if it's running east to west, you go east, if it's running north to south, you go south. But you're right, we're gonna grind up the trail. See you in Gila Bend, God willin' and the creek don't rise. We'll wait on you come the need to ride on into Mexico. Agreed?"

"We do what needs doing to bring Miss Elizabeth home. Go. I'll be along."

"Don't push that big mule too hard. You don't wanna be afoot in this country."

"I may not be fast, but I'm steady."

Ryan turned to his cousins. "Ready for the ride of your life…for Elizabeth's life? We could make Gila Bend by midnight with the help of the moon…and no accidents."

And Ryan, Garret and Reece gave heels to their mounts, leading their backups. Luckily the horses they were trailing were game and kept up. In fact, had they been turned loose, they would likely follow. But the three hard riding kin elected not to take the chance.

***

The sun had dipped below the distant horizon to the west, and the long shadows from saguaro and the few adobe and single two-story clapboard saloon-and-hotels had disappeared into muddy shadow. A mud-wagon drawn by four mules stood quiet in front of an adobe with an Arizona Territorial Express sign on the far side of the saloon, and beyond that, a lantern shone on a rough painted Conchita's Café sign with dim light on its rough windows from the inside. Maybe open, maybe not. The saloon was the single structure with a half dozen bright lantern-lit windows. The plunk of a single banjo drifted out of batwing doors of the saloon. Two whiskered miners leaned on posts outside, smoking and tipping mugs of beer. The stifling heat was beginning to wane as darkness slowly crept in. Louie and Elizabeth approached at a slow walk and Louie turned to her before they reached the saloon's hitching rails.

"Songbird, remember now, I don't fight shy of spillin' the blood of these poor dumb pilgrims, and if it comes to that, it'll be on you."

"I am so tired of the grit and grime, and smelling like a goat. All I want is a hot bath and something besides bacon, beans, hardtack and jerky."

"Don't you make no sign of distress to anyone, or you'll wish grit and grime the worst of your troubles."

"Louie, you've said it a half dozen times. Let's find that bathhouse.

"Chinee Lams, on the far side of town. Only two blocks beyond the saloon."

Two wagons, a buggy, and two dozen horses were at the rails outside the saloon, surprising as it seemed silent for such a crowd.

As they neared two men on the boardwalk, Louie tipped his hat. "Lam's still down the road?"

The man with the longest whiskers, to the middle of his chest, stepped forward. "He's got a triangle iron clanger and striker out front. Go to whackin' on it and he'll come running. He and his passel of brats live in a 'dobe out back."

"Obliged. My little wife here's about to take her quirt to me I don't get her some hot water."

"He'll whip it up to steaming in a heartbeat."

"Thanks."

They rode on, and sure as whisker's word, Lam came running when Louie clanged the triangle. The bathhouse had eight-foot-high whitewashed adobe walls and a canvas tent roof. It was divided into three three-pace rooms, a waiting area, a dressing area, and a room with two copper tubs so close bathers could hold hands were they so inclined. Next to it was another similar building but bore the sign 'Chinee Lam's Laundry and Tonsorial Pallor'.

Lam was happy to receive a half dollar with his promise to have his daughter run in with hot water every time Elizabeth called, along with all the scented lard soap the customer called for and soft towels to complete the sale.

"Thank God," Elizabeth said as she left the waiting room to the dressing area.

After she was inside a few minutes, Louie stepped up to the split in the dividing canvas, and called out. "Songbird, hand me your garments."

"What?" Elizabeth stammered.

"Split skirt, boots, blouse, and undergarments. I'm heading for the café and a swill and I'm pretty sure you won't run out into the cactus in your nakeds. Garments, please?"

"You are a black-hearted brigand, Llywelyn Bowen."

"Hand 'em out or I'll come in and get them."

A long arm appeared with gown and undergarments. "Damn you to hell."

"Pretty sure that came about long ago. How long will you be wallowing in the water?"

"Don't return for an hour."

"Likely sooner. Be here or I'll find you and parade you through Gila Bend in your natural state."

"You would. Bring me a bottle of brandy and don't forget Enano's bottle. A few beefsteaks and a dozen French croissants would be manna from heaven."

"Steak likely, one of them croissants about as likely as a fat pheasant under glass. Be here when I return."

"If you get shot dead, try and hold my clothes off to the side so they don't get holed or bloodied."

"I am touched by your concern, Songbird. Be here so I don't have to find you and hole your pretty hide."

"Humph," was all she could manage.

He rolled her garments and tied them behind her saddle. Louie led her horse back to the saloon, and noticed the small sign above the door for the first time. ALABAMA'S – FINE SIPPIN' WHISKEY– ENJOY-ABLE FEMALE COMPANIONSHIP.

As he pushed through the batwings, he was a little surprised to find the place full to the brim, not a seat vacant. Even more customers than the wagons and stock outside suggested.

Louie elbowed his way to the polished plank bar. The requisite buxom redheaded lass was pictured in a reclining oil painting over the bar. Louie was not surprised by that, but was by the fine Brunswick backbar that must have been hauled in chunks all the way from Ohio, and to add to the saloon's luster, in the center of the room was a Brunswick billiard table with two fellas circling it like wolves trying to find an opening to go for a bison's throat. At least fifty men and five barmaids watched their every move.

Louie waved one of two bartenders over. "Three fingers of something decent." The bartender poured and Louie slammed the first one down and motioned for another, as he asked, "What's so interesting about the game?"

"Best three out of five for two hundred dollars."

"The hell you say."

"I got five hundred extra on the fat man should you want to take a piece of the handlebar mustache?"

"Don't bet on horses I haven't seen run," Louie said, and slammed back another.

The place went up with a roar and applause. "That it?" Louie asked.

"That's it. Good thing you didn't bet. Fat man won."

"I need a bottle of pulque and a fine bottle of brandy."

"Pulque is a dollar and a dime. But the brandy comes dear. All the way from France."

"How dear?"

"Ten dollars the quart."

"How about seven."

"Well, sir, it's not much called for as proud as it comes, less'n some owlhoot hits a glory hole and that hasn't come in a month of Sundays. So, I'll come off a dollar."

"And I'll come up a dollar."

"And should you come up a dollar and a half, you'll own a fine bottle of French brandy."

Louie nodded, and shoved a ten-dollar gold piece across the bar as the barman fetched a small ladder and climbed to get a bottle from a high shelf of the maple backbar.

As he did, a piano and violin began a familiar lullaby from a raised stage in the very rear of the place. Even through the cigar smoke he could see an attractive woman, more conservatively dressed than the barmaids, who began to sing. And he was again surprised, as she sang beautifully.

"She a regular?" Louie asked the bartender.

"Nope, over from Phoenix. She's a local there. Ain't she something?"

"She is, but my wife makes her sound like a crow."

"The hell you say…she in the neighborhood?"

"Yep."

"How about we have ourselves a sing off?"

"I guess if this bunch has a few hundred to bet on a billiard game, they might have a few hundred to bet on a sing off?"

"I'd bet. Fact is, I'll take twenty of that my very own self."

"Fine. I'll pick the jury. Ten men at random."

The barkeep shrugged. "How much you prepared to wager?"

"Five hundred, gold coin."

"You fetch your lady and I'll announce the contest and get your five covered."

Louie shook with him. "Half hour, maybe forty-five minutes. I'll be back with the lady and the loot. But don't you be announcing 'til I've picked the jury, or no deal."

"Sounds just."

Louie downed the rest of his drink, and laughed as he left, again having to elbow his way through the crowd.

Now all he had to do was convince the Songbird.

Chapter Twenty-Three

***

"Absolutely not," Elizabeth stammered as Louie passed her clothes through the split in the canvas. "My lips are chapped and cracked, and I'm burned to a crisp and miserable."

"Absolutely for damn sure, Songbird. I got money in this. And you're clean, thanks to my good nature, and smell of lilac. Nor is that fine voice box of your'n scalded."

"My hair's wet and I can't go out in the public looking like a drowned rat."

"You're beautiful and would be if bald. You're doing this."

"Am not."

Louie was silent for a moment. "We're not going to use your real name."

"Never."

Again, he was silent a moment, then sighed deeply. "You know, Songbird, I'm getting real tired of dragging that hateful Don Mateo along. I guess I'll just shoot his chili pepper ass and leave him for the buzzards."

"They're vultures in this desert, and you wouldn't do that

as he's worth a lot of money to you. You said so yourself."

"Likely not so much as you, and the risk is much greater hauling his ass along as soon as we get in Mexico. His hundred or more vaqueros will be on the prod for him. It'd be better I just leave him to rot. Coyotes will enjoy his chops and loins."

"You wouldn't do that."

"I'd do it just to watch him squirm, and you damn well know it."

It was her turn to be silent a moment. He waited.

"Do they have an orchestra?"

He laughed. "Sure, a banjo and pianoforte make an orchestra, right?"

"Have you told them my name?"

"Hell no, they may be hunting old Louie and his new wife Elizabeth."

"Don't even say that or my throat will close up."

"I'll introduce you as...let's see...as Charlene Champaign from Sheboygan, a German countess...is that fancy enough?"

"I don't give a hoot nor a holler, just as long as it's not Elizabeth Anne Graystone."

"My word of honor—"

"For what that's worth. A chamber pot full, I imagine."

"Three songs."

"One, and you're damn lucky to get that."

"Now, wife, don't be using that kind of language."

"You 'wife' me one more time and you'll hear lots worse than damn."

"Let's go, before those louts have blown all their hard earned on rot gut and soiled doves."

"I'm tying my hair in a knot at the back. You'll just have to wait."

***

There was less moon than the night before, and as they sat on a red rock ridge with a steep descending trail ahead, Ry thought he saw some light in the distance, but couldn't be sure.

Reece stretched his arms wide and yawned, then he grumbled, "Looks like a hell of a drop off ahead. These critters are damn sure tuckered. We still got some water so let's camp here on top and rest up a little and attack the trail come sunup."

Ry shook his head. "That could be Gila Bend over yonder."

Reece snapped back, "Over yonder looks to be more'n five miles. Killing these horses or going over the edge of that steep trail should a snake rattle won't get us caught up with Kathleen…Elizabeth."

Ry turned to Garret. "Ret, what's your vote?"

"I'd let out a yell like a wee girl you touched my butt with a turkey feather. Let's water and grain these good animals, get a few hours shuteye, and tackle it come light enough to see."

"All right, I'm outvoted, but it's niggling at me, a feeling that my sis is close."

"Close, maybe, but a miss is as good as a mile and we could miss a platoon of soldiers in this dark and when we get into them salt cedars."

Reece laughed. "Ain't it those salt cedars, professor."

"Go to hell, brother. I'm too damn wore out to worry about my grammar or yours."

"True, we could easily miss them," Ry admitted. "For the stock's sake, not your blistered backside, let's move off into the brush and find a clearing. Maybe they got some steak and eggs in Gila Bend." Then he laughed and added, "Even if you gotta stand up to eat 'em."

***

Skeeter had not spent time in the desert until he climbed on his half-Percheron, half-devil donkey mule, and headed west out of Albuquerque. He'd forgotten to ask the old blacksmith-farmer the mule's name, so he had taken to just calling him 'Mule'. The critter didn't seem to mind so long as Skeeter found him water and graze.

As he didn't have a second mount as did his employer's kin, he'd taken pity on the animal, even as big as it was, and every couple of miles he'd dismounted, loosened the cinch, and walked what he figured was at least a half mile. The mule was a smart old cuss, and when Skeeter went to tighten the cinch to remount, filled his lungs. But Skeeter was wise to him, and gave him a powerhouse knee and sucked up on the cinch before Mule could fill his lungs again.

Even with Skeeter occasionally walking, they made good time as the mule had a long stride, and they'd set out well before dawn and not made camp, such as it was, until well after the hot sun had set and the desert had begun to cool.

Since his time on the plantation, where the crack of a whip was his wake-up-alarm, he'd never been much of a sleeper. And even now the soft coo of a mourning dove would bring him awake.

He was well south from the place called Vulture and he figured only twenty-five miles or so from Gila Bend, when he finally reined off the trail, headed into the brush, and staked Mule out and unrolled his bedroll. He made a small fire and fried up the last of his bacon and made himself a hardtack sandwich and chewed slowly, enjoying the cry of the nighthawk, the chirping of crickets, and the stars. So many stars, as if God had stirred a giant bonfire and sparks had boiled to the heavens. He chewed slowly, enjoying the night. He'd unrolled in a bed of dove weed, and the smell was pleasant, occluding the odor of days in the saddle without the blessing of a tub of hot water and bar of strong lye soap.

And, finally, he crawled into his two blanket bedroll and pulled the blanket up to his chin. He sighed deeply, thinking he could get used to his desert. Then suddenly sat up, cupped a big paw to his ear, and listened.

Dang if he didn't hear singing, and it wasn't no bird nor beast. A rhythmic sing-song kind of singing, and the beating of a distant drum.

And that singing sure as Hades is hot isn't English. Heathen, he'd guess. Heathen savage. He took a deep breath and contemplated rolling up and moving farther south, then decided the sounds were most of a mile away. Sound carries across a flat desert plain. No, he decided, he'd get some sleep and move on with the first morning coo of a dove or whistle of a quail.

He didn't fear the desert critters, other than snakes and scorpions, but savages were another thing.

Then he decided he was a little too comfortable and crawled out of his thin bedroll, walked to his saddlebags, and recovered the Yellowboy Winchester leaning there. It wasn't as warm as some dark-skinned, hot-blooded women he'd known on the plantation, but at the moment he thought it a particularly good bedmate. It seemed the ladies never thought him as handsome as a Nubian prince. But when he picked up a hay bale with one hand or lifted an anvil with a single hand like it was a horseshoe, and set it aside, it seemed to transform his rough features. And they wanted to conquer him with their wiles...and he didn't mind a bit.

***

The bartender stood behind the Brunswick bar,
hands resting and leaning forward, and he and a half
dozen patrons who'd seen them enter, stared. The others
were still transfixed on the blond singer. The bartender
was bareheaded, and balding, but the others snatched off
their hats. It wasn't common to see a lady in a saloon, even
a lady dressed like she was riding on a hunt. Her blouse
had a touch of frill to it, even if her split leather riding
skirt and boots showed the scuffs and wear of a long desert
crossing. She'd taken the time to put a little color on her
lips and cheeks, and smiled at the bartender when Louie
introduced her.

"I didn't believe you'd return," the bartender said, and
extended a hand to Louie and shook, but kept his eyes
on Elizabeth. As he spoke to her, he twirled the end of
the left side of a handlebar mustache, waxed to a sharp
point. "My name is Harvey P. Hanville, ma'am. Have I
heard of you, Mrs. Champaign? I believe it was…or do
I call you countess?"

"Miss Champaign will do nicely, thank you. No reason
you should have heard of me, Mr. Hanville. And it's 'miss'.
My, what a lovely voice your entertainer has."

"Your…your gentleman friend here has bet a consider-
able amount that yours is more lovely yet. Are you up for a
little competition?" But before she could answer, his gaze
shifted to Louie. "You bring the five hundred?"

Louie pulled a leather poke from his pocket and flopped
it on the bar. "Ten fifty-dollar gold pieces, all minted
in Sacramento, California, not long after the stampede.
Hard to find these days. I should be getting credit for
more per coin."

"I believe we'll just go at face value."

"Remember, I pick the ten judges at random. Any of these scamps know the lady on the stage?"

"Her manager made the arrangements. He's seated next to the pianoforte. Fella in the fancy waistcoat and bowler hat."

"Her name?" Elizabeth asked.

"Marybelle Massion, worked her way down from Chicago with that fancy-dan Frenchman booking her in places. Said she ain't never sang in no saloon, but didn't want to disappoint all the fellas who done heard she was coming. We ain't got no opera house."

"And this is her first night on stage?" Louie asked.

"Second, but she didn't hang around with all these drunks after she performed last night."

"And you've spelled out the terms to her manager?"

"I have, and the old boy smirked and looked down that Frenchy nose at me. By the by, calls himself Andre Beaulieu, or some such. I'll owe him twenty percent of my winnings. My boss over there at the faro table is covering a hundred, I've got ten, and we'll go to get others to cover soon as we announce."

Louie eyed the man across the room, barrel-chested, wearing a black cutaway coat, a waistcoat with silver thread with a four-in-hand tie puffing out at the neck, polished skin boots with a matching holster and belt tied on the outside of the coat, showing he was ready to draw. In it rested a nickel-plated revolver with flashing abalone shell grips. His hat was a medium top hat, reminiscent of Abraham Lincoln's, but half the height. But two items jumped out at Louie. He wore a patch over his left eye and most noticeably of all, a highly polished brass badge.

Louie turned to the bartender. "Am I to surmise your lawman is also a saloon proprietor?"

"Surmise?" The bartender asked quizzically.

"Yes or no," Louie snapped, then added. "Ain't he Florida Frank Hockstead?"

"One and the same. Town marshal here for more'n three months. Owned Alabama's near a year. Took the marshal's badge when our last one swigged enough laudanum to float a boat and went to sleep permanent like. Seems he was unhappy with the job and his old lady." Then he turned to Elizabeth, "And he's damn sure Miss Marybelle will take the contest hands down. Frank's been around and to lots of opera houses and heard lots of fancy singing ladies and gents."

Elizabeth gave him a dazzling smile. "I'm sure she will, but I'll do my best."

Almost as an afterthought, the bartender asked Elizabeth, "Have you been trained to sing, professionally, I mean?"

Elizabeth smiled demurely and dropped her chin, having to look up at him. "Why, sir, if you mean the church then, yes. I was taught by a lovely choirmaster. Thaddeus Jones was his name."

"I'll tell the frog we're ready."

As he walked away, Louie pulled her close and almost in a whisper, through a smile, complimented her. "Damn if you ain't getting right into this. Proud of you."

"Don't be. I only want to make sure they have no idea who I really am."

"Humph," he managed.

Chapter Twenty-Four

***

As Hanville the bartender passed the faro table, he leaned close and said something to Florida Frank Hockstead, who promptly rose and headed their way. It appeared he was well respected, or feared, as the men in the place parted and gave him plenty of room to pass.

"Welcome to Alabama's. My place." He extended a hand to Louie and eyed him carefully, through his one good eye.

"Just passing through…marshal, is it?" Louie replied.

"That, and the proud owner of this establishment. Harvey tells me your poke contains ten fifty-dollar gold pieces. Unusual these days."

"Miss Charlamain and I came from the City of the Angels. Picked them up there."

"I thought it was Champaign?"

Louie only hesitated a moment, then covered himself quickly. "No, Harvey must have been mistaken. It's Charlamain."

"And you're?"

"Willard Shortshanks," Louie said without a blink.

"I do believe we've met before, Mr. Shortshanks, but for the life of me I can't remember making the acquaintance of anyone with that handle? And I believe I'd remember."

"And where do you hail from, sir?" Louie sensed that Hockstead was suspicious. Maybe he'd read a wire about the robbery.

"Charleston." And he turned to Elizabeth. "I've been rude, Mrs. Charlamain." He gave her a short bow. "It's very nice to have you here. Like Mr. Shortshanks here, you look very familiar to me. I have had the pleasure of hearing you perform?"

"I would doubt that, sir, unless you've attended the God is Holy Baptist Church in Sheboyan."

"Never been north of Denver or Kansas City."

"Then it's unlikely. My hair is still damp from my recent ablutions and should I take a cold I could only squeal a song."

"Then best we get on with it."

"Hold on," Louie said. "Before you announce this, I have the chore of picking ten for the jury. And they'll not be betting."

"Sounds right," Hockstead said.

"You clear the bar. I want them seated there so they can't sneak in a bet."

"Will do," Hockstead said.

The first man Louie selected wore the collar of a pastor, and went to the bar, unknowing why, and took a seat. Nine more were quickly chosen after responding "no" to the question, "Do you know personally that nice young lady on the stage?"

When finished, and after explaining their purpose, Louie left the jury and led Elizabeth to the stage. They stood quietly while Miss Marybelle finished a rendition of *I'll Take*

You Home Again Kathleen, one of Elizabeth's favorites as her true name was Kathleen.

She and Louie mounted the small stage on one side, and Marybelle's manager the other, joining Marybelle in the middle.

"*Cherie,*" the manager, who called himself Andre, stopped her and explained the contest.

Elizabeth gave her a short bow. "Nice to meet you, Miss Marybelle," then turned to Andre, "*Enchante, mon ami.*"

Andre looked confused a moment and didn't answer. Elizabeth immediately got it, smiled inwardly, decided to rub a little salt in the wound. So, she smiled and said, "Miss Marybelle, *avoir un chat dans la gorge.*"

Andre nodded and said, "Of course."

He merely got a demure smile from Elizabeth, who'd said, "Miss Marybelle seems to have a frog in her throat."

Of course, no one understood. It was all she could do not to break out laughing. She'd listened carefully to the young lady and knew her range was about two and a half octaves, maybe three, while hers was nearly five. This would be no contest, if fairly judged. Of course, a saloon full of drunks were hardly quality judges of the vocal arts.

They were each to pick a favorite song, which both would sing. Then the judges would select a song which both would sing.

To Elizabeth's slight surprise, Marybelle picked a Confederate marching song, *The Bonnie Blue Flag,* which may be a smart choice as most those wandering Arizona territory were expatriate rebels, in fact most those now wandering the west. It certainly wasn't a regular in Elizabeth's extensive repertoire, but she knew it well enough and if Marybelle went first, she'd pick up the rest. Elizabeth, on the other hand, picked *Ave Maria,* which the piano and banjo players immediately complained they didn't know, to which Elizabeth announced she'd sing acapella. Marybelle then admitted she didn't know the words so Elizabeth said, "That's fine. You pick another you'd like and I'll sing *Ave Maria* in both English and Latin."

Marybelle went pale, and Andre began to mutter that it was not the deal. Louie laughed loud enough so the audience could hear, and asked, "So, you are afraid to pick another song of your choosing. I'd think you'd relish—"

And the crowd, now taking interest, began to chide the phony Frenchman. And Elizabeth asked, "*Tu viens d'où?*"

It was the simplest of questions, "Where are you from?"

He began to turn red in the face. Then almost shouted at Marybelle, without responding to Elizabeth, "Pick a damn song, Cherie. I am going to the bar."

"No, you're not," Louie challenged. "You're not going near the judges."

Andre turned crimson. "Sir, I'll have you know—"

"I know plenty," Louie said, his hand resting on the butt of his revolver.

Hockstead, who stood just below with one boot up on the low makeshift stage, spoke up. "Andre, take a seat down here next to me and I'll buy you a drink."

Sputtering, Andre left the stage and Louie followed. But Louie, as was his custom, walked to the side and leaned against the wall where he could observe not only the stage but everyone in the room.

Marybelle sang a nice rendition of *The Bonnie Blue Flag* and got a rousing, foot-stomping, and standing ovation from the mostly southern crowd of drunks.

Elizabeth picked up enough of the words to get through the song, only adding a couple of interesting and difficult trills, enough to receive an equally enthusiastic response.

Then it was her turn to go first. She began *Ave Marie* in English, and as she expected, the rather raucous crowd became more and more quiet. By the time she'd finished, tears actually streaked a few dust-covered miners' cheeks. Then she began a rendition in the original Latin, a normal verse, then a verse an octave higher. The crowd was mesmerized. There was dead silence for a moment, then she feared that the applause, foot-stomping, and cheers would bring the building down on top of them.

She bowed a time or two, and turned to see Marybelle stomping off the stage.

She smiled at Louie. "It seems Miss Marybelle has retired. I so wanted to tell her how much I enjoyed her range and elocution."

Louie waved her to join them as he and Hockstead elbowed through the crowd to join the judges, who merely shrugged. "Looks like a default to us," the man in the pastor collar said as soon as they reached the bar.

Hockstead yelled over the noise to Harvey, "Give the man his winnin's." And the bartender handed Louie back his pouch, only this time nearly full.

"Now, friend," Hockstead said, "How about you and I step outside? I know now where I've seen your lady friend and she's no Miss Charlamain. I believe she's Elizabeth Anne Greyson. In fact, I know she is after hearing her sing."

Louie smiled a tight-lipped snake grin. It faded as the lawman, standing close, rested a hand on Louie's gun butt.

"Gonna be hard to pull that iron, Bowen, with me resting my paw on it. Move your hand away and I'm gonna lift it out and you're coming peaceful-like. As of the wire this morning, you're worth a thousand dollars to me. You might notice my bartender has a coach gun aimed to cut you in half, you decide to make trouble."

Chapter Twenty-Five

***

The sheriff's right hand rested on his own holstered revolver, his left atop Louie's still holstered six-shooter. Just as Elizabeth reached them, Louie spun the sheriff so he was between him and the bartender's shotgun. All those at the bar and behind the two men scrambled for cover, as Louie came out of his pants pocket with the derringer and put one shot through the big man's back exiting his barrel chest, then shoved him up hard against the bar before he could sag. Harvey, the bartender tried to jump to the side to get a clear shot at Louie, but even if he had one, hesitated as he'd likely take out three customers as well with the sawed-off barrel.

Harvey hesitated far too long as Louie's second shot took the bartender in the mouth, and he was quickly laying across the backbar, blood gushing onto his perfect handlebar mustache as he sank slowly to the floor.

Louie had his revolver in hand and realized Elizabeth was scampering for the batwing doors, easily done as half the crowd was running in front of her clearing a path.

"Songbird!" Louie yelled.

She was stacked up against ten miners and drovers and

townsmen trying to force their way through the doors. She spun on a heel and glared at Louie.

He shrugged as his gaze swept the remaining crowd, making sure no one else was interested in making a play. It seemed not, so he turned his attention back to Elizabeth, who now was striding his way. As soon as she got within reach, she slapped him hard enough that his ears rung.

"Damn you, damn you, damn you," she yelled with a stomp.

"Pull in your horns, Songbird. Ol' fancy Frank gave me no choice. I know who Florida Frank is…was…and he's got ten or more notches on his grips and half of them was shot in the back, if rumor is true. So, they ain't gonna be no tears dripping on his grave. Now let's beat a trail before another of these pilgrims gets ambitious…besides, he recognized your singing and was about to announce who you was…and I promised that wouldn't happen. I done shot him for you."

"And you're a liar as well as a murderer. Where's Enano's bottle?"

"Damn Enano's bottle."

"I'm not going peacefully unless you take Enano his bottle. I don't want to see you having to shoot the little man."

Louie waved his revolver at the men lining the wall across the saloon as he strode around the bar and grabbed two bottles.

"I hope you're happy. Now you made a thief outta me."

Her eyes rolled and she shook her head as she spun on a heel and headed for the batwings.

She said over her shoulder, "You want a clear conscience? Leave a couple of gold pieces on the bar."

"Hell with that! I wasted good lead on Florida Frank

and that bar soap. It's a fair trade."

She pushed her way through the now clear doors, shaking her head in disgust as she went.

***

Don Mateo was on his butt with his legs stretched out, on the only clear sandy spot in sight. His bloody wrists bound behind, his teeth clamped in anger. He'd had enough, and wondered if he'd ever be left alone with the little man again. They were nearing the border. He was exhausted. He was angry. He was hungry. He hadn't been allowed to relieve himself since Louie Bowen and the woman had ridden away. Worse than anything as far as he was concerned was he was beginning to doubt the woman. She hadn't whispered "escape" to him in the last two days. Was she beginning to enjoy the *bastardo's* company, this Louie Bowen? Don Mateo was through waiting for an opportunity without greater danger.

The little man was strong for his size, and seemed more than proficient with both revolver and rifle. That was the bad news. The good was he'd found a bottle of Who Hit John bourbon in Bowen's saddlebag, and even though only half full, it was plenty to make the midget slur his words and stumble. Maybe he was now careless? *Dios* will provide.

It was as dark as a Sinaloa *juzgado* dungeon, the moon just gaining courage to peek over the distant eastern mountain range, and he presumed Louie and the woman would soon return. Soon return even if they'd treated themselves to a fat steak in Gila Bend.

"*Señor* Enano, I must relieve myself."

"Ha, piss your pants, *haciendado*," Enano slurred from his seat on a pile of saddles, then slurped the last of what must have been a pint of whisky in the quart bottle.

"You have been an honorable man this far...not like that *bastardo gringo*. Have you no mercy for a fellow *pisano*? Do you wish to smell what I must put in my *calzoneras* if you do not find mercy in your heart, while you follow on the trail? The Apache or the Yaqui will smell us from two miles away. I have asked little of you. I have not cheated you of a visit to the *pueblo*, of a bottle of pulque, of a bowl of *carne asada*, of a tender *señorita*. That was the *gringo,* not me, Enano."

"You...you try to pluck...to pluck the strings of my heart, *haciendado*. I am not so easily fooled."

"Fooled, no, but used? Of that there is no question. You allow the *gringo* to take the woman. He is likely in a hotel room as we speak, making her squeal with pleasure while he grunts like a rutting *cerdo*." Don Mateo managed to get to his knees as he could see the little man's face was reddening. His anger might make him careless. "Then again, maybe you are the fool."

"I will show you who the fool," he said, and stumbled toward Don Mateo with both small hands knotted into fists.

On his knees, Don Mateo was the same height as Enano. As Enano neared, his fist cocked and ready to try and break Don Mateo's nose, he came a little too close. Even with his wrists bound behind, Don Mateo had a weapon he'd often used, and he threw his head back as if afraid of the blow. Then slammed forward, head butting Enano with all the force he could muster. Already wavering, Enano hit the ground on his back, his nose spraying blood, and he covered it with both hands. Don Mateo fell to his back, swing his legs to the front, over Enano. With all his strong vaquero legs could muster, he beat Enano with his booted heels, knocking the breath from him, then moving up, knocking him unconscious as he smashed heel after heel into his face and forehead.

When he was sure the little man was unconscious, Don Mateo struggled to his knees, then got to his feet. Angry, full of a meanness that scorched his backbone, even with wrists bound behind, he kicked the little man in the ribs, once, twice, and a third time that rolled him onto a low paddle of a tuna cactus.

Now, to loosen his bindings, free himself and saddle his *caballo*. He was tempted to await the *gringo* and use Enano's weapons to spill the *bastardo's* blood on the sand. To rescue the woman. But she had done him no favors of late and he was unsure of her.

Now, to free himself, and escape into the night. He relieved Enano of his knife, and began to saw his bindings.

He had to clear the opening in order to get to his mount, but bare-handed wouldn't work with the spines and thorns of the cactus used to block the opening. He ran to Enano again, who had a pair of gloves looped through his belt, then laughed sardonically at himself as he couldn't get four fingers inside. So, he removed the little man's belt and then looped it to lasso the paddles of tuna and spires of cholla.

He was only halfway into the pile when he heard the rattle of hooves on rocks in the distance. He abandoned the horses, gathered Enano's Colt, a handful of jerky, and hard biscuits from a stack resting near the fire. Then he charged south into the thick salt cedars. Jamming the Colt into his belt, he moved south, then would turn east. East to Gila Bend and the law, and a mount.

He was soon punctured with spines trying to move through the low cactus shaded by salt cedars, but he charged on.

If Louie Bowen chased him, the Colt would open the man up. In fact, Don Mateo almost hoped he would.

Chapter Twenty-Six

***

"Damn that greaser," **Louie said as he dismount-**ed next to Enano and sunk to his knees. Then he exclaimed, "He's still alive."

"But unconscious," Elizabeth said, placing a palm on the little man's forehead. "Water, maybe. Give me your can."

Louie untied the Army canteen hanging behind the cantle of his saddle and handed it over. Elizabeth freed the hanky stuffed into her belt, wet it, and mopped Enano's face. He didn't wake, but moaned.

Louie walked to the edge of the camp and studied the ground. "He headed south, but he knows his only chance is Gila Bend." Then he walked back and studied the woman for a moment. "I'm going after him."

"I'll stay and tend to Enano."

"Yes, you will. Give me your boots."

"What?"

"Give me your boots."

"I won't try and escape. Enano needs my care."

"Boots."

"You are six kinds of a son of a bitch, Louie Bowen."

"Boots."

She moved to a rock, sat, and began removing her knee-high doeskin boots. Then she threw them at him. He laughed and gathered them up and stuffed them in his saddlebag. He mounted, then said quietly, "Those thorns and spines will keep you away from the stock. If you have a smidgen of compassion you'll care for Enano. He was as good to you as could be expected. Grab up them gloves of his and hand them over."

Elizabeth walked over and searched the ground until she found both gloves then handed them to Louie. "These won't fit you."

"But they might fit you and I wouldn't want you to get full of spine pricks tugging on that fine fence Enano built."

"I hope Don Mateo is already in Gila Bend."

"If I'm any kind of a tracker, and I damn sure am, he went out of here right in front of our arriving. Otherwise, he'd have forked his gelding."

"I can still hope…"

"Hope is a waking dream, Songbird."

She glared at him a moment, then risked a comment. "Poe?"

"I'm surprised at you." Louie laughed. "Nope, that ol' Greek, Aristotle."

"If you're so bloody smart, why do you act as you do?"

"Just do as I say. Keep a low fire, if any. You wouldn't look so good chewing hides in a wickiup."

"Wickiup?"

"Just keep a low fire." And he reined away, not the way Don Mateo's tracks had left, but rather to the east, back the way they'd come, leading Elizabeth's palomino.

She watched him leave, shrugged, then returned to

mopping Enano's forehead again.

Louie rode the hundred yards back to the two-track express company trail, then east for over a quarter mile to an arroyo, bottomed by a wide gravel and rock-strewn river bed that must have been a wandering branch of the Gila when overflowing its banks, then he turned south in the center of the fifty-yard-wide wash. He moved a couple of hundred yards off the road, then reined up and sat quiet.

If the Mexican was trying to make Gila Bend, he'd have to cross this wide clearing, and coming through the underbrush he'd be easily heard, or seen in the moonlight. Louie hadn't sat for more than a quarter hour, when he heard rocks roll as something moved down the bank into the ravine bottom. Louie slipped his Winchester from its scabbard and lay it across his thighs, then quietly gigged his Morgan forward until he figured he was forty yards from where the man was crossing.

He waited quietly until a man stumbled into the wash, and to its center, before he called out, "*Haciendado*, I suggest you sling that six-shooter of Enano's far away and sink to your knees and pray I don't put one in your belly for causin' me all this trouble."

Don Mateo hesitated only a moment, then drew the weapon stuffed in his belt and fired quickly. Not bad, Louie thought, as the shot buzzed by an ear. The Mexican got off another that went wide also as Louie shouldered the Winchester and fired, holding his aim low.

The *haciendado's* right leg flew out from under him and he tumbled to his belly, then rolled to his back, and yelling Spanish words even Louie had never heard. He then sat up and tried to aim the Colt again.

Louie yelled out. "You wanna spill all your innards on

this river bed? You fire another one at me. Throw the
weapon far as you can chuck it, or the next one stops your
corazón from beating, black as it is."

Don Mateo cursed again, but flung the Colt to the side.

Elizabeth was tiptoeing around the camp in her stock-
ing-feet when Louie clomped back in, leading Don Mateo
on Elizabeth's palomino. Elizabeth was disappointed, then
a little frightened as she realized Don Mateo's right leg was
clamped with a tourniquet—his own belt—and was soaked
with blood below.

"What happened?"

"He done run into one of my .44/40s. Dumb greaser."

"Get him down, damn you."

"Don't be damning me, be damning him. He cut loose
on me. You damn near lost your riding partner and he's
lucky it wasn't his backbone I blowed out."

"Get him down. I've got to tend his wound. He's lost
a lot of blood."

Louie unloaded him and laid him beside Enano.

Elizabeth snaked a knife out of Enano's belt sheath and
cut a flap in Don Mateo's bloody *calzoneras*. Having to be
careful not to fill her own hands with the forest of spines
covering his leather trousers. She lay the flap aside.

"Through and through. God willing, missed the bone
if I'm any judge. I have a needle and spool of strong silk
thread in my reticula. It's still seeping, tighten that belt."

"Yes, ma'am," Louie said with a laugh. Then he
turned serious as he did as requested. "We won't be
crossin' the Sonoran draggin' two gimpy, sickly, sad
excuses for mankind."

She gave him a phony smile. "Then why not drop the
three of us off in Gila Bend? You may not be welcome there

but we'd get along."

"Same chance of that as a snowball would have in them embers. Sew him up and let's get some sleep. I got a friend just aways south in the Crater Range, near White Tanks. She's half wolf-bitch and half witchwoman, cooks better than a New Orleans hotel chef, pokes better than a New Orleans Cajun whore, and will put us up and mend these hooligans faster than a falcon can dive on a grasshopper mouse."

"Mr. Bowen, you make a scum-sucking pig look classy. Please keep your exploits to yourself. Now, get that belt off before he loses a leg. Does this witch have a tub?" Elizabeth asked as she worked. She finished Don Mateo's wounds, having to pack the exit wound on the back of his leg as a chunk of flesh half the size of her fist was blown away. Then she turned Enano over, and as suspected, he had a gash where his head rested on a jagged stone. She cleaned the cut as well as was possible, and applied a dozen stitches to the wound. Then she turned her attention back to Louie, who'd boiled some coffee and sat watching her work.

"Better," Louie said.

"Better what?" Elizabeth questioned.

"Better than a tub. She's a fine one with claw feet in her quarters, but she's got a hot spring and we can take us a dip."

"We? I'd rather smell like a ten-day-dead corpse than bathe with you."

"Don't you worry, Songbird. Aracela will take care of my needs. Hell, and she can even sing like an angel."

"Aracela? A pretty name for a witch."

"And a pretty witch she is. Just hope she doesn't put a hex on you."

"I'm exhausted. We'll worry about hexes some other time. Please, watch over these two while I get a couple of hours of sleep. I think we have Don Mateo's bleeding stopped. I presume Enano has a concussion. If he awakens, don't let him go back to sleep and wake me. On your honor?"

"Ha, I think I remember you saying I had no honor."

"Just do it, *bandito*."

"Go to sleep, Songbird. I'll wake you. Two hours."

Chapter Twenty-Seven

***

Ry had them up well before sunup, and to his great surprise, just as they were brewing one more pot of coffee before mounting up and riding out, Skeeter came clomping into camp.

Ry gave him the best grin he could muster this early. "By all that's holy, man, you must have ridden the night through."

"Got me a couple of hours. Somewhere out yonder from my camp, them savages was singing and carrying on. I figured I'd get the jump on them just in case they had my curly hair in mind."

"I just wiped the skillet out, but we got time to fry you a little bacon."

"Let's ramble on. It's been a'itching my backbone that we're some close to Miss Elizabeth."

"Skeeter, you're my kind of pard. Let's ride."

It took them an hour to descend to the salt cedar flat, then they set the animals into a lope. Gila Bend was no more than five miles distant.

***

It took Louie and Elizabeth longer than usual to break camp. Enano had finally come to sometime after midnight, but was, of course, dizzy and had a terrible headache.

They tied Don Mateo, strapping his legs to the latigo to keep him from tumbling out of the saddle. He was weak, probably because of blood loss. Louie took sympathy on him and bound his wrists loosely in front, taking a couple of half-hitches around the saddle horn with six inches of play on either side.

Enano had been talking to himself, rattling in Spanish, ever since he'd come to. He said over and over, "Don Mateo, *muerto, muerto, muerto.*" Elizabeth knew enough Spanish to know he was saying "dead, dead, dead." He repeatedly insisted the Louie return his Colt, after Enano had mounted, and he did.

As soon as Louie returned to his own mount, Enano slipped his Colt from his holster, leveled it on Don Mateo's back, cocked it, and pulled the trigger.

The resounding "click" rang across the camp.

Louie looked over this shoulder. "Enano, you are reckless with that bag of money we call Don Mateo. I unloaded your weapon and it will stay unloaded unless we are attacked or until you come to your senses. Your head is muddled. Understand?"

Enano merely mumbled, "Don Mateo *muerto.*"

Louie shook his head. "He may die anyway, but it won't be due to your recklessness."

"Enano, please!" Elizabeth said.

Louie had redone the string, handing Elizabeth the mule's lead rope, stringing the two packhorses behind his mount.

As they were about to string out toward the two-track, Louie pulled rein and turned back to the others. "Quiet. *Silencio.*"

"What?" Elizabeth asked.

"Quiet, damn you!" Louie snapped.

They sat quietly, until the mule brayed.

"Jerk his damn lead rope," Louie said, as loud as he dared.

Elizabeth did so and the mule stopped his noisy bawl.

The Elizabeth realized why Louie had demanded silence.

Hoofbeats, several animals at a lope, on the two-track only a hundred or so yards from where they rested.

"Silence, could be savages," Louie said in a loud whisper.

As they passed, and Elizabeth realized the riders were disappearing toward Gila Bend, then she realized the occasional clang of a horseshoe on a rock certainly didn't indicate unshod Indian horses.

"That's not Indians," Elizabeth chastised.

"Can't be too damn careful," Louie said and gave her a dismissive glance.

She was tempted to give heels to her palomino and try to overtake the riders, but she'd have to outrun Louie and his tall Morgan Chestnut, and then Don Mateo would likely try and escape and Louie would run him down, and this time the shot might not be to the leg.

***

Ry, Garret, Reece and Skeeter, only four miles from Gila Bend, with their minds on steak and eggs, loped by tracks leaving the trail. They were hard to see in the hardscrabble among the thick salt cedar and low cactus. He heard one bray from deep in the brush, but with wild asses running free in the desert, thought little of it.

They rode into the little town and directly to the Alabama Saloon and reined up in front of the adjacent café, hosting a small sign that read "Alabama Grub Club", and it was full of miners, stockmen, and city folk.

They all walked in together. The walls above the generous number of windows sported horns: elk, buffalo, mule deer and antelope. Pelts hung on walls between the windows and draped the benches outside. All the tables were full, with only two seats at a long dozen seat counter, and they were divided by a large fella in a bright red linsey-woolsey shirt and black twill trousers, ragged over scuffed boots.

The man behind the counter was carrying a green porcelain coffee pot that was at least a gallon large. Ry turned to the other three. "Flip until it's odd man out, then again. Them left standing gets the vacant seats."

They each dug a coin out of their pockets and flipped. Reece was the only tails and shrugged and moved on outside where the two pelt covered benches flanked the door. Another round and Ret had the only heads. He shrugged and followed his brother.

Ry slapped Skeeter on the back. "Guess it's you and I, pard." They walked to the counter and Ry tapped the man between the empty seats on the shoulder. "Hey, friend, would you mind slippin' over so I can jaw with my friend?"

"No problem," he said, then turned far enough to see Skeeter. Then he turned back to his meal and continued forking in eggs and beans.

"No problem?" Ry repeated.

Without bothering to turn again, the man snapped. "Ain't moving for no shiny black skinned Ethiopian. Did you read the sign?" And he motioned to a sign that said, **"No Africans or Indians. Tables out back for them and our Mexican neighbors**."

"No problem," Skeeter said. "I'm too hungry to whip half these fellas. I'll go—"

"The hell you will," Ry said, his jaw clamping and heat flooding his backbone. He grabbed the big fella's shoulders and jerked him back off the stool. He landed hard, flat on his back with an audible "oof," his head bouncing once on the hardwood floor and once into Ry's hard fist that bounced it again. On this bounce, it returned spurting blood out of both nostrils. His eyes rolled up, and he lay limp, indicating his unconscious state.

The big man with the coffee pot rounded the end of the corner, yelling, "Take that outside or I'll scald the hide off'n you."

Ry's voice dropped an octave as he whipped his Colt up. "Friend, that boiling coffee is a deadly weapon, we don't take to being threatened with deadly weapons. You take another stride and the next cup you swill will come spurting out the holes in your fat belly."

The man slid to a stop, eyes widening, mouth flopping open, one hand extended palm out, wanting nothing to do with the Colt.

The place had gone dead silent, as all eyes turned to the weapon in hand, and before Ry could speak again both Reece and Ret pushed back inside. "Problem?" Reece asked.

Ry smiled. "The big ugly galoot in the apron threatened to scald us with hot coffee. Seems he's offended by the coffee color of our pard."

The waiter or cook or whatever he was still held the steaming pot with one hand, and fortunately no one was seated behind him as he was directly in front of the opening he'd charged through.

Reece, faster than a lizard could suck up a fly with his long tongue, drew and fired, holing the pot, which sprayed coffee from both entry and exit holes.

Half the place began to quickly empty out a side door and back through the kitchen.

Chapter Twenty-Eight

***

Skeeter whipped his hat off and stood before the man. "Y'all got room for four out back?"

"Got room for a dozen," he muttered, never taking his eyes off of Ry's weapon. His hand was shaking, making the pot dance a little.

"Thru that there door?" Skeeter asked, pointing at a side door.

"That's the way," the aproned man said, but his eyes remained on Reece's six gun, then he seemed to relax as Reece slipped it back into his holster.

"Make it five outside," Ry said, then added, "bring along his fixin's when you get time." He motioned to Skeeter then to the man. "You want to gather him up." And Skeeter bent, grabbed the unconscious diner under the arms, hoisting him over a shoulder as if he was a sack of grain, and yelled to Reece and Garret, "Y'all mind eating out with the colored folks."

Both gave him a smile. Then Garret spoke up. "Too damn smoky inside."

So, Skeeter continued, "Would y'all catch the door?"

They both laughed and headed over and opened the side door.

Ry turned to the shaken man, still holding the draining coffee pot, "Friend, are you the proprietor?"

"Nope."

"May I speak to him. Seems we owe him for a pot and the contents."

"He's dead. Louie Bowen kilt him over next door, just last night."

Ry was silent for a couple of seconds, then asked. "He still about? Bowen, I mean. In jail maybe?"

"Seems no one had the guts to try and take him there."

"How'd you know it was Bowen?"

"More'n one of the fellas drinking in the saloon recognized him."

"So, maybe he had a room in the hotel?"

"Nope, rode out with his lady friend after shootin' Harvey Handley, the bartender and Frank Hockstead, who owns this place...owned...and the saloon, whorehouse, and hotel next door...and was our city marshal. Bowen shot 'em both dead as an anvil. Then lit out."

"Headed out which way?"

"West."

"On the Express Company road."

"That's the only one west."

"This woman he was with. Did she seem distressed?"

"Not so you'd notice. They had them a sing off with another lady entertainer. Won a pocket full of gold. This woman went by Charmain or some such. Sang like the best whatever graced the San Francisco opera...not that I never been to no opera."

Ry sighed deeply, then dug in a pocket and came out with a two-dollar gold piece and slapped it on the counter.

"That's for the pot and the coffee and a tip for your trouble. Sorry about the blood on the floor and the hole in the wall. We'll eat now, out back. I'm a generous tipper, friend, but if you spit in our food it'll be the last goober you roll over your tongue. It's a dollar tip for good food and fair service, and an ounce of lead should we feel slighted. Got it."

He looked offended. "I take care of my customers. All of them. That was Hockstead's rule about coloreds out back. Fact is, I'm a squaw man myself so it always got my hackles up."

"Steak and eggs, potatoes, biscuits, a plate a foot high in flapjacks, honey and real maple syrup you got some... and keep the coffee coming. Four hungry hands and a guest, and the four of us done rode all the way from the big canyon of the Colorado. And, by the by, I'm paying for the fella's breakfast whose head we used to test the strength of your floor."

"Yes, sir. How'd you want them steaks?"

"Hot through. Just cook the moo out of 'em."

Ry walked out and plopped down at the table.

He eyed his kin. "She was here last night. Rode out west with Bowen, after he shot a couple of local fellas dead in the saloon next door. Seems one of them was the city marshal and owned the saloon and this café."

"Humph," Reece managed, and Garret merely stared at him a moment. Ry cut his eyes down and studied his hands, not meeting their gaze.

The big fella in the red shirt had come to and was tearing pieces out of his shirttail to stuff in his nostrils to quell the bleeding. He and the kin seemed to have already come to terms and made friends. He'd even shaken with Skeeter. He was so friendly they'd returned the little but deadly .45 caliber Sheriff's Model Colt to him.

Ry eyed him. "Sorry about the misunderstanding, friend. But Skeeter here is like kin to us and we couldn't let you anger him. Big as you are, you ain't much more than half of him and he'd jerk one of your arms off and beat you dead with it. Were it to come to that, we'd be stuck here for a trial and your funeral."

The big fella merely nodded, then extended a scarred and knotted paw to Ry. "Theo McTavish."

Ryan introduced himself, then added, "The ol' boy in the apron is fetching your breakfast out here. Pleased to have you join us and pleased to buy your breakfast, and another should you still be hungry. What's your profession, if you don't mind me asking?"

"Don't mind at all. I'm a prospector, been hunting this desert over for a glory hole."

"Well, good luck to you. You know this country well?"

"Every snake hole and rocky precipice, from Yuma to the White Sands, from the Sea of Cortez to the Colorado River Canyon...the Grand they've gone to calling it. I been at it, dodging the Yaqui, Navajo, and Apache for years. Afore that I was with Crook, cooking and packing for the Army."

"With him a long time," Ry asked.

"Since Virginia and Army of the Kanawha, then fought the Snake and Paiute at Tearass Plain with him, then the Modoc up in Californy, then Yavapai here in the territory. I mustered out after the Skeleton Cave Massacre. Didn't have the stomach for it no longer. At that tangle we killed over seventy, from papooses to full-growed braves. It was enough for this pilgrim."

"So, you've been wandering around here a couple of years?"

"I guess that be right. Seems like a hundred at times."

"Turn up any color?"

"That's a question you don't ask a prospector, my new young friend. Even if you are standing him to steak and eggs."

Ry laughed. "Sorry, didn't know the rules. You ever think of guiding other folks?"

"Why would I guide other folks to find a glory hole—"

"Not our quest. We're after an outlaw name of Louie Bowen."

"Saw him and saw some posters on him. He's worth a thousand to him has the sand to take him down…dead or alive. A hard case, that Bowen. I was in the Alabama last night. He's close. I still have the fine lilac scent of his lady in my proboscis."

Ry clamped his jaw at that. "I was told—"

The aproned man and a young Mexican or Indian girl arrived with their arms full of plates and began distributing them.

Ry instructed him. "Another steak and eggs for Mr. McTavish here."

"Burned black, as usual," McTavish instructed.

Ry continued. "It's reported he rode out to the west. You tie up with us and a fifth of the reward is yours."

McTavish eyed him skeptically, "And two dollars a day and found no matter we find him or not?"

"Done," Ry said, extending a hand. "You don't mind riding with some of Lee's boys?"

"War's long over, thank the good Lord. I'm afoot, 'cept for my donkey," McTavish informed him.

"We'll solve that at the local hostler."

"Ain't selling my donkey. She's close as a sister to me."

Ry laughed again. "I'll pay the hostler corral and board for two weeks and she can have a vacation. You got a weapon?"

"I got a shiny new '73 and a scattergun."

"Good enough," Ry said, and glanced at his kin and Skeeter to make sure he got no objection. And got none.

McTavish again extended a hand and shook.

"Eat," Reece snapped at both of them. "Let's ride that Welsh son of a bitch to ground." Then he asked, and his tone not friendly, "Ry, did you ask if she was lovin' up to this Bowen? Are we chasing a will-o-the-wisp who doesn't want to be caught, or kidnapped kin?"

Ry reddened, then through clamped teeth, growled, "If Kathleen…Elizabeth…hasn't cut his nuts off yet it's 'cause she's just biding her time. If you want to ride back north, it's on you. But if you hang with the kin, and you impinge my little sis's character again, I'll shove that Colt of your'n where the sun don't shine."

Garret spoke up as the two of them stared at each other across the table. "Both of you shut your pie holes. We'll hear it from her own words soon enough. Eat, we're burning daylight."

Chapter Twenty-Nine

***

"You've got to slow down," Elizabeth commanded with a strained shout.

Louie was moving at a cantor. He glanced back over his shoulder, and reined up. They were well out of the salt cedars and the country was becoming more and more sparse with only the occasional patch of sand, peppered with greasewood and the occasional mesquite or stringy smoke tree. Hardpan, flat sandstone, occasional floats of ancient volcanic rock, black as a foot up a bull's butt, faced them for as far as they could see.

Elizabeth dismounted and checked Don Mateo's leg, which had stopped weeping, and the ties keeping both he and Enano in the saddle. Enano had occasionally lifted his head and looked around. The saddle horn had to be bruising him badly as he, from time to time, lay over it and it pounded him high on his chest as his mount strode to keep up. Louie had removed their bridles and tied them behind his saddle and let the animals run free, tying their lead ropes around their own necks.

Louie reined back beside her as she remounted and spat

the words at him. "You're going to kill both of them if you keep up this pace."

"You're right. I'm going to kill both of them…but only if they can't keep up this pace. Is that what you want?"

"And if we come upon more savages? I thought Enano was valuable to you. And Don Mateo is worth a fat pouch of gold you said. How far is this witchwoman?"

"Six, maybe eight miles more. Two hours if we keep moving."

"Then another hour will make little difference. A brisk walk, please."

"They may have a posse rounded up in Gila Bend, and after us even now. They will never find Aracela's castle. The first time I was there I was led in with a blindfold. Even the Yaqui fear going near. So, we continue the lope. We'll be on hardpan and lava soon. Then an Apache couldn't track us."

"You'll kill them."

"It's God's will," Louie said, "if they die. If they die, they die. *Que sera, sera.*"

"You are truly a bastard."

"And if you continue to besmirch my sainted mother, you'll feel the bite of the quirt on your backside, and I may have to pull down that split riding skirt to do a proper job."

"And I may have to find a rock while you sleep, and discover if there are any brains in that ugly noggin of yours."

"Just ride, Songbird, and dream of a hot spring to soak your weary bones."

***

Ry, Garret, Reece, Skeeter and their newly hired guide, McTavish, were working their way back west on the express company road. They'd purchased a sixteen-hand dappled gray for McTavish as his primary mount, and a skunk-striped dun mule as his back up. McClellan saddles, former army issue, and Army saddlebags were cheap now that thousands were everywhere in the west, so he made do with tack he was familiar with.

They moved at a slow walk, studying the flanks of the road for signs of riders turning off either north or south. Soon after passing a wide arroyo, McTavish let out a whoop.

"Here, two shod animals headed south off the road. Clear as if a pollywog was swimmin' in your beer."

"Damn if I didn't hear a donkey or mule bray when we were riding in. I thought it was a wild critter. You don't suppose we were that close and missed them."

Garret laughed. "Too bad cuz wasn't practicing her singing."

"Or singing to that new beau of hers." Reece said.

Ry ignored him. "What's south of here?"

"Mexico, and the toughest damn country twixt here and there ever tortured man and beast."

"Must be some civilization?" Reece questioned.

"Mexico, if you can call that civilization. More and more it's Yaqui country. I've worked it hard looking for a volcanic blowhole that might be lined with the yellow metal, but even if one was discovered it would take a consortium of rich folks to get it out. You could build a smelter but you'd have to haul in the wood, and they ain't enough water most places to fill a pan."

"Then why bother?" Ry asked.

"Well, sir, a couple of saddlebags full of nuggets pried outta the sidewalls would keep me in bacon and beans and a beautiful *señorita* for the rest of my days."

They kept riding into the salt cedar, avoiding the spotted

cactus patches as they tracked.

"So, they have to find water to cross the Sonoran lava flats?" Ry asked.

"They do. I bet it tops 100 degrees today. I know of three oases, two a little brackish but potable and usually approachable. The third I've never been able to get to as each time I got within a couple of hundred yards of a cut leading into some rocky spires…in some low rocky mountains called the Crater Range, near Two Toad Tanks. Them tanks are poison. You can usually tell bad water as skeletons are scattered about. But on a cold morning I've seen steam working its way out of a cut deeper in the Craters, and someone is damn jealous of the spot. I could never get close. Every time I neared, a warning shot cut over my head too damn close for comfort. One time I yelled out, "*Amigo, agua, por favor*," but the shooter had no sympathy for a dry throat, and all I got was a closer shot. I hightailed it, dragging Matilda."

"Matilda?" Ry asked.

"That sweet little donkey we left back in Gila Bend."

Ry couldn't help but laugh.

"That was over a year ago they shot at me…or near me. It's likely sweet water—nobody would shoot a fella over poison, I don't imagine—and a hot spring or it wouldn't go to steaming."

"And the other two?"

"Dead Squaw Wells, which is two pools each about fifty feet across on a sandstone flat. Good water, but not enough wood about to boil a pot of coffee. And Mantequilla Hole, a pool in a canyon of rock yellow and smooth as butter. Higher up the canyon walls are some smoke trees and some cedars. All them places are to be approached like you was crawling into a rattler's den. Apache and Yaqui use them to cross the lava flats and it ain't wise to contest the savage, particularly in his backyard."

They clomped into a small clearing, with a fire ring and blackened logs with a whisper of smoke rising.

Ryan shook his head. "Damn, damn, damn. They were here. Looks to me like they had friends. Seven or eight head of stock, all shod." Ry leaped from the saddle and walked a ring around the camp. "Headed out of here south. I bet they worked their way over to the big wash. How's the river to cross there?"

"This time of year," McTavish answered, "she's a hundred yards wide and knee deep. No hill for a stepper."

Ry bent and pulled a rag out of the fire. It was covered with blood. "Somebody is hurt. Bowen didn't take a shot last night, did he?"

"No, hell, he was the only one got a shot off."

"Let's ride," Reece snapped. "I'll bet whoever this is, is not five or six hours ahead."

***

The country was sparse, only the occasional sa-guaro, and cholla, different cholla that was stubby and fat, spines thick as a hedgehog, unlike the ones farther north. They neared a small range of rocky spires, the black ones obviously volcanic, still rough and hard as the hubs of hell, but interspersed with reddish sandstone smoothed by the wind and occasional water, very occasional.

"Crater Mountains," Louie announced and pointed at the strange mixture of structures. The sandstone even had a few through-and-through holes, a couple as big as a pair of Conestoga wagons piled one on the other.

Louie reined up a half mile from the nearest outcropping, slipped his Winchester from its saddle scabbard and fired two shots, one quickly following the other, then a third well after those two. He reseated the rifle, and they plodded on, this time at the brusque walk Elizabeth had suggested miles back. Don Mateo seemed to be in great pain, but moved along with teeth gritted. Enano was fully awake, but it seemed his anger far exceeded his headache. He glowered at Don Mateo constantly.

Louie pulled rein again, only a quarter mile from where Elizabeth could see a wide breach in the sandstone rock. It appeared to have a flat bottom, ten or more paces across, where a stream exited the little range, she surmised. Little rain graced the territory, except for the occasional monsoon, when gully washers would carry a man and horse away were they not careful to stay to the high ground.

As they neared, a man wearing a wide sombrero stepped out of hiding a hundred feet high in the rocks. Louie doffed his hat at the man, but he merely watched them approach.

Louie turned and gave her a wide grin. "They know me here, but might shoot you just for the hell of it."

"If they know you, they'd have shot you long ago. Where's that hot spring?"

Louie merely laughed, and they plodded on into the cut and welcome shade of the high cliffs on either side.

Chapter Thirty

***

They worked their way over a quarter mile into the mountains between high slick cliffs, but it was an easy ride on the slowly climbing stream bed. Then it opened into a quarter-mile-wide sandy flat probably a mile long. Two men in sombreros and serapes waited, as if expecting them. Off to her right was a trickle of a waterfall, hardly any volume but over one hundred feet high, beginning at a ledge high above, ending in a pond with a foot-wide stream leading only fifty feet away into the sand, where it was eaten by the desert. She was more than a little astounded to see a dozen cottonwood trees in the flat, a few more than two feet in diameter. It was a clean flat, as all downed wood had long ago gone the way of campfires.

Had she had time to relax and study her surroundings she'd think it more than a little mystical, as the sun painted the walls and crevices in shadows and reflections, and only then for a short time as the walls were high and occluding.

"*Señor* Bowen," one of them said, touching the brim of his hat.

"*Señora* Aracela is in her nest?"

"*Sí*, I will take you up."

Louie turned to the second man, pointing at Doc Mateo and Enano. "Treat them tenderly. Do not give my small friend any ammunition for his revolver as he is angry with the other. The tall one is my prisoner, and wounded. Unload him and make sure the wound in his leg is not bleeding, and that he doesn't try to crawl away like the snake he is. Unsaddle and water the stock. Make both my prisoner and my *compadre* a bed from the saddle blankets. In the shade. Apart from each other as they have a feud." Then he handed the man a five-dollar gold piece and got a grin showing two missing front teeth, surrounded by brown and black ones that would likely soon join those absent, all under a bushy, untended, mustache.

Then he helped Elizabeth out of the saddle. She sighed deeply and let him put a hand to each armpit and lower her.

"You tired of the saddle?" Louie asked her with a grin.

"If you touched my…my bottom-side…with a powder puff, I'd cry for a week."

"My, my, the way you talk, Songbird. I know you're tired of riding. Soon you'll be tired of climbing."

She eyed him and gritted her teeth. "What I'm going to do is go over where that man is making a bed of sweat-wet saddle blankets, lay down, and sleep until someone brings me a cold lemonade and a charcuterie, with extra brie and prosciutto."

Louie laughed. "I don't know a char…whatever you called it…but you might be surprised what Aracela will have up in her Eagle's nest. But we gotta climb a bit."

"I'm no rock climber," Elizabeth groused. Then she thought of her small valise, still, she was happy to note, tied securely on the mule's pack. "And I must have my small case if I'm to dress properly. How am I to get it up a cliff?"

"Stairs, Songbird. Been cut and built in that stone mountain over there since Methuselah was a whelp…long before I'd guess. Let's go. She's got a castle and a cave so deep it keeps things cool, and a hot springs that'd boil a chicken should you throw it in near the source. But I ain't gonna carry no case up there."

"Then," she said, adamantly, "I will carry it."

"No, you won't. I'll have them haul it up on the hoist."

"That's safe, I hope?"

He laughed. "They haul kegs of whiskey down, so I'd guess they could haul your little case up."

"Fine, and I don't need a keg of whiskey. I'll settle for a cool drink of water. If we gotta climb, let's get started."

"Two hundred eleven stone steps. I usually stop halfway. I'll stop every forty steps since you're a tender lady."

"You didn't act that way when you kept giving heels to that big Morgan."

"You gonna gab the day away, or follow me and *Señor* Sombrero here to a fine bed and some of the best grub in the territory." He turned to the man staying with his charges. "I'll send down some food and drink for those two on the rope. And, *amigo*, it's for those two, not you. See they get their fill." He turned to Elizabeth. "They got a rope hoist for supplies and such."

The man shrugged, looking a little offended, but then nodded.

"Lead me to the stairs," Elizabeth said.

The Mexican in the huge sombrero took the lead. Elizabeth was only slightly shocked when the guard raised his Winchester to the sky and fired two quick shots, then another a couple of seconds later.

Louie gave her a grin. "You might have gotten your pretty head shot clean off if the top didn't get that signal."

It was an eerie climb, twice passing through wind holes in the red rock, often passing ancient petroglyphs of faded orange, black and yellow, many merely handprints, some of antelope, buffalo, or deer; some of animals that no longer existed in the desert. Many times, there was a precipice only a foot to the right, so high that the plunge would give you time to think over the sins of your life before it was extinguished.

She stopped more than once, not because she was exhausted, but to admire the work of ancients. They finally topped the rock edifice and were fifty yards across the flat from the semblance of a castle, two stories, constructed of both stone and adobe, with ramparts to match many English and Scottish country homes she'd visited. It had a verandah across the front, shaded by a canopy, not of silk or canvas, but of woven blankets or rugs common to the Mexicans and Indians. Pots and baskets, some with dried desert plant arrangements protruding, some with planted cacti or succulents, lined the front. But the most obvious decoration was a woman in a bright red gown, wide sunbonnet, with black lace covering her face.

Elizabeth stood, catching her breath, taking in what she considered an amazing accomplishment so high in the rocks.

She rose, in a regal manner, as they approached, but did not remove the lace veil.

Bowen whipped off his hat. "Aracela, you're very kind to receive some weary travelers."

"You have always been a pleasure to entertain, Louie Bowen, and will be again should your lady friend not interfere with our amusements."

"She's more of an investment than a friend. Can we trouble you for some sustenance for the two of us and two more in the care of your castle guard down in the castle keep?"

"What kind of hostess would I be, Louie me lad, if I refused weary travelers?"

"Is she Irish?" Elizabeth asked.

"I am right here, missy, should you have questions of who I am, where I've been, or where I'm going…should any of us have an answer to a quandary such as our destination in life."

Elizabeth gave her a brilliant smile, now that she'd caught her breath from the arduous climb, and offered, "I'm sorry. That was rude. Aracela, if I may. Or I'd be happy to use your full name or a proper title, should I be entrusted with one?"

"Aracela will do nicely. I left titles behind more than that a decade ago, with the death of my dearly departed who discovered and constructed this oasis. Now, enter my humble abode and let's see how my distillers have done with the last batch."

"Distillers?" Elizabeth questioned. "You distill your own whiskey?"

"Dew of the angels…or dew of the devil, depending upon your view of things. Fact is, miss…I did not catch your name." And she turned to Louie. "It is not like you to be so rude."

Louie laughed. "Miss Elizabeth Anne Graystone, it's my great honor and pleasure to introduce you to Queen Aracela, mistress of the desert, proprietor of Castile Aguila, and the best damn cook this side of Paris."

"Thank you," Aracela said with a smile that showed even through her lace veil.

"My pleasure. You mentioned a new batch?"

"Please, follow me." She stepped aside to allow Elizabeth to enter, as Louie pulled aside a door as thick as his hand was wide. As Elizabeth passed, she asked, "Are you related to, or are you, the singer of some repute?"

"I am her. And another dubious accomplishment is added to my curriculum vitae…I'm a very unwilling prisoner of your friend Louie Bowen, held, I presume, for ransom. At your service, Miss Aracela."

The hostess ignored Elizabeth's rather caustic remarks, then smiled and offered, "I play a fair dulcimer, actually a German guzheng, but few know it by that name. Perhaps we could enjoy each other's talents after supper. Not that mine are one-tenth of yours."

"That would be enjoyable, and in your case, I will gladly sing for my supper," Elizabeth said, not wanting to insult her hostess. Particularly one who might provide a fine meal, a real bed and a soapy soak in a hot spring.

"You must be exhausted, following this incorrigible Welshman across the desert most think of as hellish. I'll show you to your accommodations." Then she turned to Louie. "Separate accommodations, I presume."

"You presume correctly. As I said, an investment of which I have no interest in depreciating."

She laughed. "I've heard it called many things, but never 'depreciating'." He joined her laugh and then continued. "Then I'll have Paco bring your saddlebags to my room, and hers to hers."

Normally Elizabeth would have feigned a blush at that, but she was too tired to feign.

"As I'd hoped," he said, then added. "The latest batch?"

After they'd finished tasting Aracela's new batch of pulque, of Tequila, and of whiskey distilled from a beer brewed from some desert seeds the source of which she would not divulge, she showed Elizabeth to an upstairs room.

As they walked, Elizabeth questioned her, as if interested but actually to judge her odds of escaping.

"I saw no distillery. How do you accomplish that task with just a couple of men and your servant ladies?"

Aracela studied her a moment before answering, as if deciding if there was any danger in giving away her secrets, then obviously decided little if none. "We have a village of a dozen adobes, some families, on the far end of the flat down below. I have twenty *hombres*, a hundred dray animals, a dozen freight wagons. Many of my employees tend the works, many are guards. All are marksmen and have often had to defend our home. We proudly possess a Gatling gun and a mountain howitzer, a brass field piece, both of which the savage has learned, the hard way, to respect. The Yaqui and Apache had use of this place before we came, and have often had to be discouraged from returning."

Then she sighed deeply. "I've never abided killing until I saw what the savage was capable of, and they had me captive for more than a year so I was witness to more than one atrocity."

Then she continued with her story and Elizabeth was quickly convinced Aracela was proud, rightfully so, of what she'd accomplished. "We use the heat of the mountain, which escapes as steam inside one of the caverns. We need no wood so it's very efficient. The stills are in the caverns. Other caverns are cold, so ideal storage. Our only disadvantage is hauling in oak for our barrels but we have an excellent cooper, who was a shipwright in Vera Cruz before joining us. We are very protective of our mountain, which is why we let no one approach. My husband, now deceased, was an Irishman, a prospector when he stumbled upon this place, and recognized it as the treasure it is, God rest his drunken soul."

Elizabeth couldn't help but smile. "We all have our talents…and our faults."

"Yes," Aracela replied, "but, like many men, his talent for the jug even exceeded his talent for creating his own poison. Still, I don't mind selling it all over the territory. We will ship two hundred kegs of whiskey, over one hundred each of pulque and tequila, and for the first time this year twenty-five kegs of gin made from our own desert juniper… what many call cedars hereabouts. Most think Arizona juniper unsuitable for the brew, but Mr. O'Reilly found a way to make it digestible."

"How did you befriend Louie?"

"We would have shot him out of the saddle as when he first arrived as he ignored the warning shots we fire at anyone approaching. But he was laying across the withers of his horse and just kept coming. As it happened, he was wounded, in and out of consciousness, and his horse more concerned with the smell of water than the sound of gunfire. We nursed him back to health and he amused me. He could have stayed, but Louie Bowen is not the staying kind. Seems his roots have always grown shallow So, I welcome him back from time to time, as amuses whichever of us is in the mood to be amused. He's ninety-five percent man and only five percent rat."

They shared a laugh at that.

The room was cool, as only thick rock walls could achieve, and had a separate toilet room with a privy hole above a shaft descending its two-story height to a hole of un-known depth just as in a European medieval castle. There was also a fine side table of some highly polished Mexican hardwood, laden with a water-filled white porcelain pitcher resting in a matching bowl. The mirror over the table was rimmed with gold leaf, and best of all, the bed was wide and deep in throws so thick they could only be goose down, and they were in turn covered with a half dozen pillows equally soft and puffy. Best of all, her valise had been hauled up and lay on the bed.

She eyed it all, almost drooled, and actually swooned, before she turned to Aracela, "I'm astonished and so very thankful. May I have a couple of hours before we dine?"

"We dine as they do in Spain. It will be at ten o'clock. I will awaken you in four hours, if that suits you?"

"You are an angel."

"Hardly, but I am a decent hostess, unless you displease me."

She'd overcome the temptation of asking why she never removed the veil, still wondering if the woman was not dangerous, and maybe jealous of Louie's charms, such as they were. Elizabeth closed and slipped a bolt on the door, too tired to be as concerned with Aracela's last comment as she might have been. Probably should have been.

The last thing she did before falling into a deep sleep was check the false bottom of the valise for her jewels, and far more important to her, the broach her mother had willed her.

It was all there.

Chapter Thirty-One

***

They lost all sign of the trail by the time the sun was directly, fiercely, overhead, then headed for the most likely destination. Mantequilla Hole was a half-acre recess in a small outcropping of yellow rock, and the water smelled somewhat of sulfur, but not so much to be poison. The only tracks thereabouts were of a few unshod horses—maybe wild, maybe Indian—some javelina, a few deer, and that of vultures and quail. Even elk didn't bother to come this far into the flatland.

They headed out for Dead Squaw Wells on a flat that could be surveyed from more than a mile away. They saw from a long distance that no one was near the water hole, but still needed to be reassured, so rode to the edge of the pool. The hard ground gave up little in the way of tracks near the water, but the pool was almost centered in a treeless bubble of hard yellow rock in the desert. They separated and rode the circumference of the nearly mile-long and half-mile-wide blister of yellow rock.

No shod horse tracks anywhere.

They moved on toward the water—only presumed to be

there by McTavish—in the small Crater Mountain Range. It was near sundown when they came upon the track of seven shod horses as they approached the water source McTavish had never seen, guarded by someone he'd never seen. The place that harbored a shooter seeming more than willing to send approaching strangers to meet their maker.

They followed that track until they were only a mile from the cut into the hard-shouldered rocks that rose steeply from the desert floor as if shoved up out of the sand by an unseen but powerful hand: The Crater Range.

"Parlay time," Ry said, and they gathered up—Five men, ten head of horses, and enough arms to start a border war.

When together, Ry addressed McTavish, "Track is headed directly at the cut into the Crater Range. How about one of us ride right at them, innocent like, and see if we draw fire? If we do, we reconnoiter the mountains looking for another way in, and then, even if we have to go head on, wait until dark when they can't see us coming. If they are shooting at passersby, they got something to hide. Even if they're not harboring Bowen and Elizabeth, it might be interesting to see what's so valuable it needs gunfire to protect."

Reece spoke up, "If it's not Elizabeth and thousand-dollar-Bowen, I don't give a hoot. Whoever follows this track in should make sure it doesn't turn south again, like gunfire shied them away like it did you. That's first. Second, if not, we try and find another way in as I don't want no sharpshooter working on his game with me as the practice target. Even in the dark, we could be riding into a couple of guards who could lay down on us from twenty feet. That doesn't take a sharpshooter. Only a dumb chili-head with a scattergun. Agreed?"

All of them nodded. So, Reece continued, "Who wants to be the Judas goat and draw fire?"

Garret laughed. "The Judas goat is ofttimes the only one to live through as he leads the others to slaughter, so I don't mind wandering in to see if there's still an owlhoot with a sour attitude."

"Hell with that," Ry said. "It's odd man out again. Last two will call match or not. Last man standing goes."

They all reached for a coin.

After several rounds of flipping coins, Ry won, or lost depending upon your view of things, the honor to ride until someone tried to scare him away, or if in a bad mood, shoot him out of the saddle.

He clomped along, leaving his second mount with the others. Only occasionally did he glance down to see if he was still tracking the seven animals, one of which he hoped was ridden by his sister and another by the bandit who might be a bonus of one thousand dollars.

As he figured he was nearing the two-hundred-yard mark from the entrance, he watched for the puff of smoke from a rifle, knowing he'd have to duck before he heard the report. Rifle fire, he knew, traveled faster than sound, but not sight

There was a shadowed cleft with an indentation that could be a trail, at least one hundred feet above what had to be the bed of an occasional stream, a stream that had likely created the canyon, and he kept his gaze there. The most obvious....

He was barely able to flinch as a billow of white smoke proceeded the buzz of a lead hornet over his head. He straightened, quieted his mount, who'd sidestepped nervously, then removed his hat and waved it as if greeting some unknown shooter.

His greeting was answered by another shot, this one closer. He spun the gray he rode, and gigged him into a gallop back the way he'd come.

He slowed to a walk after a quarter mile. Joining up with the others at more than a half mile of an additional brisk walk, he was quick to announce. "Tracks kept heading right for that split in the mountains. Let's stay as low as possible and split up. I judge this little range to be four miles long. Don't know how deep—"

"'Bout two miles, half as deep as long," McTavish said. "I been all around it, stickin' my nose in a couple of places. Lava says volcano, and volcano ofttimes means the yellow metal, sometimes even diamonds. However, with the lead flying, if'n I had to guess I'd say this is the filthy lair of the lowlife, a hideout for the lowest outlaw scum and this Louie Bowen was welcomed in."

"So, do you think there's another way in?"

"There's a two-track on the far side, opposite this opening. Last I was here about it looked like many a wagon had come and gone. I tried to head in thataway, and dang if some no account didn't take a pot shot at me. I decided right then and there if they was shootin' at casual folks they'd already laid claim to anything worth working. Hell of it is, last time I was in Prescott I took a look in the claims office and there was nothing filed in the Crater's. Could be they don't want to stir up a rush, but who knows. The other side of that coin is you may be right. It may be an owlhoot roost."

Ry removed his wide-brimmed hat and scratched his head, then said, "Skeeter, how about you, Reece and Ret go left and see what you can see? McTavish and I will head to the right. Let's circle this little range and meet on the other side. Agreed?"

Garret added, "Don't pass this two-track should you come to it, that way we won't miss each other. Let's stay at least a half mile from the mountains so we don't alert whoever is making a lair of the place."

"Let's go! Dark is bearing down on us," Reece said, and spun his mount to the right.

Ry yelled after them, "Hey, kin, don't get dead out there. I might need a little help if there's more than a dozen of them."

"Likewise," Garret yelled over his shoulder as they set out in a brisk walk.

Chapter Thirty-Two

***

Most of the way that encircled the Crater Range was thick enough with stands of Mesquite, Saguro, and thick cholla that they were not easily observed from the mountain. Picking their way around took them over an hour to meet up again. They arrived within a quarter mile of each other on the two-track.

When they joined up Ry was the first to speak up. "Y'all see anything looked like a way in…where we might pass unseen?"

Reece quickly replied, "Don't know if you could see it coming your way, but this road leads to a village, *pueblo* I guess they call it around here. Maybe ten, fifteen of them adobe huts, some corrals and what not. Interesting, the approach is fenced fort-like. Gun towers on the two corners, manned. Big double gate. I don't think they want company coming from this way any more than the other."

"Maybe we ought to send a test rider near," Ret suggested.

"Hell with it," Ry said. "Let's not alert them anyone's about. Let's make camp. A hundred yards back is a wash that's a dozen feet below the desert floor. Small fire won't be seen. We can watch the road from there, more'n a mile back as it comes this way, and if we put a man up on top of that little knob back yonder, he can survey the fort or whatever it is."

Skeeter had been quiet for the last two days, going along with whatever the kin decided to do. He was used to paying heed to the white man so it troubled him little…but he now sensed he was close to his employer, close to the woman who'd treated him fairly, far more fairly than any white person had ever done, the woman who'd made him near whole again with an expensive limb to replace the one he'd lost. So, he didn't ask for council, merely stated what he had in mind.

"Y'all, I'm gonna put the sneak on that village and get me lots closer so's I can figure a way inside. Looks to me like a fella might climb up that there fissure on the north side and maybe work his way around the cliff and be over them houses so he can see what they be up to."

Ry sensed there was no need arguing with the big man, so he suggested, "Skeeter, that wooden peg of yours might be fine for kicking some *bandito* in the head bone, but I don't imagine climbing cliffs is one of your long suits. If you want to get close and see what's up, good enough, but taking a tumble off that steep face and through the roof of one of their adobes would likely let them know someone is about and maybe mischief is at hand. How about we all do our own recon and meet back here at midnight?"

Skeeter gave him a nod. "Well, sir, I sure ain't the tree climber I used to be. But I can't sit and wait thinking Miss Elizabeth might be giving up on anyone coming to help her. I'll go about my business and be back here come midnight."

"Be careful."

Skeeter mounted his big black mule and headed off toward the pueblo.

The sun had dropped behind the Crater range, and they'd been in shadow for a half hour. There would be little daylight left, but then darkness was likely now their friend.

Ret and Reece headed for their animals and swung up into the saddle. And Reece yelled at Ryan, "About a mile back is a slot canyon leading up into the mountain. We eyeballed it and it's likely too damn steep for man or beast but it's worth a closer look."

Ry gave him a nod and yelled after him, "We may have a long night. McTavish and I didn't see a damn thing worth following up on. We'll get some chow ready and see you back here come midnight."

The brothers waved over their shoulders and gigged their horses into a lope and disappeared to the north.

Ryan and McTavish found a spot nearby to make a quick camp, a deep indentation into the ravine wall that soon became a corral, made from the dry husks of saguaro and strung reatas, for their animals and the spare stock, then they got some beans boiling and bacon frying. Just as a pot of coffee was beginning to perk, Ryan put a finger to his lips and shushed McTavish, then asked in a loud whisper, "You hear that?"

"Sounds like a wagon. Maybe two."

"Let's flank the road. This may be our ticket to the party. Don't move unless I do, understand?"

"Yes, sir. You move and I'll back your play."

Ry grabbed his Winchester and McTavish a scattergun and they ran for the road. They took positions out of sight on either side of the two-track, well before the wagons neared. If there were few, they'd make their move; if too many, they'd stay hidden.

It was twilight, barely enough light to see, when the wagon party clomped into sight. Two men on horseback, likely guards, but with rifles in scabbards and not at the ready, rode ahead of two wagons. The wagons had only a driver on each, four men total.

Both the riders and drivers appeared to be half asleep as they neared. The horses and drove teams knew where they were going and needed no rein on the familiar trip.

As they drew even, Ry decided this was just too good an opportunity, and charged out of the brush. His Winchester wasn't shouldered; rather, he held the barrel, making a cudgel of the stock. He swung it hard and caught the guard on his side on the back of his head, just below his sombrero.

He pitched forward out of the saddle. The other guard seemed to think his *compadre* had fallen out of the saddle and reached for him to keep him from falling, then was surprised when McTavish grabbed his reins with one hand and jammed the barrels of the scattergun into his side with the other. He jerked rein on the man's mount so hard it backed into the team of the wagon immediately behind, and caused that team to back up and crash into the one following. The drivers were so busy trying to control their teams they could pay little attention to Ryan and McTavish, or the fact both guards were out of the saddle and face down on the two-track, now both unconscious as McTavish had jerked his man out of the saddle and pistol-whipped him.

Ryan ran for the wagon in the rear and had a hand on the near horse's headstall and his rifle leveled and centered on the driver, who was reaching for a weapon under the seat, but Ryan's stern "No!" caused the man to stop and raise both hands.

In less than a minute both drivers were on their knees in the road beside their senseless friends, the teams and horses quiet, and Ryan and McTavish standing with rifle and shotgun in total control.

"You speak their lingo?" Ryan asked the prospector.

"Enough to order grub and find the pisser. Some more, not much."

"Let's get them trussed up and over to camp. Garret's the professor and linguist of our bunch. Damned if we don't have us a ticket to the party, as there's no doubt in my mind them fellas at that gate yonder are expecting these fellas to arrive...now it's just if we want to go."

"Up to you all. I'm ready for a bowl of *frejoles*."

Chapter Thirty-Three

***

Ryan and McTavish heard brush busting and stepped back into cover, rifles at the ready, then a voice rang out, "Hello the camp!" Reece's voice.

Skeeter, Reece and Ret returned about the same time. Dismounting, Reece stood studying the four Mexicans bound hand and foot, the extra riding horses, and the two wagons and teams that had been driven off the road near the camp.

"Dinner guests?" Reece asked.

Ry gave him a hard smile. "Not sure they wanted to join us, but McTavish and I were pretty insistent."

"What's on your mind?" Garret asked.

"First, did you find anything promising?"

Garret shrugged, "The slot canyon climbs too steep for stock. We could likely go in afoot but it's near two miles from it to this one that's guarded fore and aft. It would take us all night and day to get up there and over this far. And climbing in the dark would be damn dangerous. Then we'd be afoot with only what we could carry. Who are these fellas?" he said, waving at the bound Mexicans.

Ry shrugged. "You got their lingo. We were waiting on you to do some interrogation. I'll twist their ears, or some worse, they don't answer up. By the way, circle marks in the wagon beds says they were hauling kegs out, and by God if they weren't bringing some useful supplies back."

"Useful?" Garret asked with more interest.

"Maybe. Two cases of dynamite, boxes of fuse detonators, a whole case of .44/.40 ammo, and lots of pantry goods…flour, sugar, coffee, and what not."

"Well, we aren't thieves, but let's find out what's going on in there. Twist their tails if need be."

As Garret walked over to socialize with the trussed-up guards and teamsters, Ry turned to Skeeter. "You see anything of interest?"

"There be one fella in each of them towers at the edge of the wall. I did the creep and crawl up near, then some hounds went to barkin' and I backed off. But before that I did spot what has to be a hell of a big ol' cave 'bout fifty or sixty feet up the cliff a half mile south of the village. Them ol' bats started flying out of a hole up there and just kept on coming. I'll bet there was a million or more. Blocked the stars that was just beginning to show."

"Interesting."

"And there was another pouring out bats, but it was inside the canyon some past the village."

"Connected, you think?"

"No way to tell."

Garret was engaging one of the teamsters in what appeared to be friendly palaver, considering the man was hogtied.

After a stint as a sharpshooter, Garret had been an intelligence officer in the signal corps and spent much of the war trying to decipher Union flag signals, in addition to interrogating prisoners who might have knowledge of the same. He'd been trained in gathering information and in fact had at one time been sent into a confederate prison as a spy, impersonating a prisoner, to eavesdrop and befriend a cell full of signal officers.

As a professor, and after spending a year in each country, Garret had taught both French and Spanish prior to the war.

Before he began questioning in earnest, he insisted they separate the men, and questioned each out of ear-shot of the others.

Reece and Skeeter were just scraping tin plates of beans with chunks of hardtack when he returned and poured himself a cup of coffee.

"What?" Ryan asked.

Garret shook his head, somewhat astonished. "Damn if each of them didn't have the same story. Whiskey is the story."

"What?" Ry asked, furrowing his brow.

"Seems they got stills up in some caves. They use steam from volcanic vents to drive them. None of them know a thing about the Welshman and his woman—"

Ry snapped, "She ain't his woman."

Ret laughed. "The Welshman and some woman, but said they wouldn't know for a week if they entered the split in the hills on the other side, it's near two miles over to what they called the west gate."

"So, if Elizabeth came in the west gate?"

"Eagle Castle, Castile Aguila, is the roost of the *jefe*, the boss woman, a widow woman, who runs the whole oper-ation. Seems she distills whiskey, and brews both pulque and tequila, which is what this outfit is all about. Lives in a rock house, built like a small castle, five hundred or so feet up on a flat on the west side."

Ry pressed, "And…I can tell by the coy smirk of yours there's lots more?"

"She has a *gringo* friend. A *bandito Americano*. But he comes and goes and they don't know if he's come again."

"How many are in this village?"

"About fifty, including women and children. Only sixteen men on this end and a half dozen on the west end. Three guards always on the bottom, one up on the flat near the house, and a cook and houseboy."

"Guards won't be expecting interlopers from this end," Ryan observed.

"So, let's get inside and get things secured, then head for the other end. I don't guess they got one of them fancy new elevators?"

"Stairs, and a rope affair to raise and lower supplies. But it's shanks mare to the lair."

"Word was Louie was mounted on a tall chestnut and last seen Elizabeth on a palomino. If they still got the midget with them, he'll be easy to spot. And if this Don Mateo is still a prisoner, as was surmised all the way back in Prescott, he's likely to be trussed up. So, it's past these fellas in the pueblo, past a couple or three guards on the other end, climb a couple of hundred feet of stairs out in the open, and storm the castle. Hell, we should be done by lunch tomorrow."

Reece laughed. "Sounds easy as storming Old Round Top. I'd suggest we truss these fellows up in the back of the wagons. Cover them up with their own tarps. Borrow their sombreros, and ride on in. With luck there will only be a man or two at the gate. They can join their amigos in the back of the wagons, and presuming this road goes all the way to the west side—"

"It does," Ret assured him, "I cleared that up right off."

"Then we just keep riding," Ry said, "and take care of the guards on the west side, and call on the lady *jefe*."

"*Señora* Aracela O'Reilly, believe it or not."

"Let's hope she enjoys visitors," Reece said.

Ry shrugged. "Lady hasn't offered up much of a welcome so far."

"Well, sir, I guess we'll have to give the lady a lesson in southern hospitality."

Chapter Thirty-Four

***

Elizabeth was rested. She had her sass back.
Aracela had rapped on her door—the woman was still
veiled, a mystery—at half past eight and to her great
surprise when she opened the door, handed her a yellow
gown that felt like silk, and fresh underthings. As well as
a Spanish tortoiseshell tiara and a beautiful yellow cactus
flower. She was accompanied by a rotund Mexican girl
carrying a bucket of steaming water with towels draped
over her pudgy shoulders.

"Miss Elizabeth, this is Adoncia. She will bathe you, then
help you with your hair and fit the dress." She handed over
a pair of black low-heeled shoes, nicely shined, and a pair
of black silk stockings. "I judged you as size six, so these
may be a tad large. You will offend no one in your bare
or stockinged feet if you prefer. Your leather skirt, soiled
clothes, and boots are being cleaned. I took the liberty of
relieving you of them while you slept. You have an hour
and a half before we dine, but there is a nice Sangria and we
can enjoy the stars a while on the veranda if you're early."

"I will be, particularly with Adoncia's help. I can't

thank you too much."

"It's my pleasure. I look forward to some sophisticated company. Louie is good company, but after all, he is a man."

"At times too much so for his own good."

Aracela's light mood seemed to darken. "And what, exactly, do you mean by that?"

"I only mean he seems eager to prove he's the cock of the walk…to use his fists or his firearm to get what he wants."

"Ahh, on that we can agree. However, this is a hard land and it takes hard men."

"He is that. I have a favor to ask?"

"Please."

"The little man, Enano, and another prisoner of Louie's are under guard down below. Both injured. I wouldn't want the little man to try and negotiate your stairs as he likely has a concussion and would surely tumble off the edge, and the other, Don Mateo, has a gunshot—"

"Don Mateo?" she asked, seeming to know him.

"Yes, he was on the same stage as I and was taken prisoner by Bowen."

She collected herself, shaking off her surprise. "Go on."

"He has a gunshot wound to the thigh. Both need care, fresh dressings, and food and drink. And be careful, they are a danger to each other."

"I'll send Adoncia down when you're through with her. She can be back in time to serve our supper."

"Thank you. You're very kind."

"I have my moments," she said, and closed the door.

As soon as she was gone, Elizabeth removed the night-gown that she had found earlier in a dresser drawer, and enjoyed standing near the bucket as Adoncia scrubbed her down, water flowing freely onto the rock floor and out a scupper in the wall. Her Spanish was limited, but she made herself known with "*qué es*" and sign language when she inquired about the veil.

"*Cicatriz,*" said the chubby girl.

"*Cicatriz?* Scar?"

"*Sí,* scar." And the girl ran a finger from beside her eye all the way to her chin.

"Sad," Elizabeth said under her breath.

***

Elizabeth was almost breathless at the sight of the long carved, polished table, set only on one end for the three of them. Silver chargers and water goblets, crystal Champaign flutes, heavy silverware, napkin rings carved from elk horns, and meat knives were set at each place setting with elk horn handles, all of it set off by Chinese entre and salad plates, each set individually and intricately hand painted to match. All laid on a silk Chinese embroidered tablecloth that reached nearly to the floor on all sides. Enough cloth to serve as a jib sail on a small sloop. And the table would seat at least a dozen.

"Never," Elizabeth complimented Aracela, "have I seen anything outside of Europe, and I have been in such places as the palace of the Emperor of Austria-Hungary, that excels what you've created here."

"You're too kind, but I too traveled, and a forty-foot table with solid gold settings, like what is offered other royalty at Schönbrunn Palace in Vienna, dwarfs my humble attempts."

Elizabeth eyed her with some curiosity, then as her flute was filled, asked, "How long have you been ensconced in this most interesting abode?"

"I lost my husband in a steamship explosion on the Rhine in Germany, and was injured and scarred. I returned here, my traveling days over, and suppose I'll die here."

"Scars don't offend me, Miss Aracela, if you're more comfortable without the veil?"

Aracela sighed deeply. "I suppose I should say kind of you; however, I'd prefer we continue the mystery."

"Of course. So, you'd been here sometime, I suppose, if you afforded travel?"

"Sean O'Reilly was a miner. He'd worked the Crater Range out of gold and silver, and gotten very rich, then realized his played-out workings would drive a distillery. He'd been treated badly in the States...you know, no Irish need apply...and nearly died of yellow fever working the plantations, the horrid swamps, in Louisiana...treated badly, more so even than the slaves. He was fine with his Mexicans, who loved him and now love me, and never seeing the arrogance of the east again."

Louie, at the head of the table, had been taking all this in, swinging his head from one to the other, and seemed more than merely a little bored. "You said something about some kinda bird?"

"Hungry, Louie? Well, we shouldn't leave the man of the house...at the moment...waiting." She turned to a doorway and raised her voice a little. "Adoncia, aperitif and our first course, *por favor.*"

As equally surprised as she had been with the table settings, Elizabeth's chin almost dropped to her chest when a plate of raw oysters was served on a bed of greens.

"We are far from the sea?" Elizabeth remarked as she dipped a bite size morsel in a red sauce, then winced a little as it was pepper hot. It seemed to her that the nearer the border, the more pepper hot all the food.

"The oysters cost little. The wagon load of ice to get them here, after being hauled all the way from Oregon, cost a great deal. Fortunately, we are able to enjoy iced drinks for a short while after they arrive."

Both Adoncia and the fat cook, Fidelio, had to carry in the main course—a beautifully browned, stuffed, sandhill crane. Its gray-feathered wings, tail, and long stretched out neck decorated a five-foot-long silver platter, and the breast and body were surrounded by root vegetables which were, in turn, flanked by cactus flowers. All was complimented by the bird's brilliant red-feathered cheek plates.

"Oh, my!" Elizabeth managed. "I don't believe I've ever enjoyed crane."

"It is the finest of North American birds," Aracela said, with a satisfied smile.

"Much too beautiful to eat as it graces your beautiful table," Elizabeth said.

"Bullshit," Louie snapped, "tear me off a chunk."

"Mr. Bowen," Aracela, said, her voice a little low and ominous, "I have a guest, and unless you want me to feed you to the hogs, you'll mind your manners."

Bowen cut his eyes at her. "I'll have a leg and thigh, O'Reilly."

Elizabeth realized that even though he hardly showed his inebriated state, he must have been enjoying Aracela's free and plentiful whiskey the whole time Elizabeth slept.

Aracela glared at him a moment, then turned to Adoncia, waiting attentively in the doorway. "Please carve Mr. Bowen a leg and thigh, and serve him the sides. That's for his stomach. Even though he's obviously partaken to an excess, pour him a goblet of whiskey for his attitude. Perhaps it will encourage his retirement." Then she gave Elizabeth a seemingly sincere smile. "Do you have a preference?"

"Never having enjoyed the sandhill, I'll leave it up to you."

"Please carve a bit of both breast and the remaining thigh for my guest and myself."

Every glance of Aracela's toward Louie, while they ate, showed animosity.

For the first time, Elizabeth wondered if Aracela might be her escape from Louie's clutches.

After they finished a small bowl of chocolate and clotted cream, they retired to the veranda. Aracela instructed Adoncia to fetch her German guzheng, and while Louie continued to drink, played and sang.

Both of them knew a songbook full of Irish folk songs, and as soon as they realized it angered Louie, sang one after another.

He finally stomped off and sat on a rock near the several-hundred-foot cliff that was only fifty yards west of the castle, and drank alone.

Chapter Thirty-Five

***

The kin spent two hours gathering graze for their extra stock and preparing the wagons with all their weapons, distributing scatterguns and rifles with boxes of .44/40s under each. They bound the two guards and two freighters tightly and left them face down and hogtied. Ry and Reece, who was the best shot and fastest with his sidearm, took the lead on horseback, side by side in the guard's position. Ret drove the lead wagon, McTavish the second, and Skeeter lay in the bed of the trailing wagon, covered with the tarp up to his neck, as he was far bigger than any of the four Mexicans and might be noticed.

At three AM, they set out at a slow pace, approaching the double gate, a single coal oil lamp hung from a crossbeam fifteen feet in the air, five feet above the rock walls. No lights shone in the turrets on the corners or at any of the gun-ports spaced ten feet apart in the walls.

They saw no one, but as if willed from above, a gate swung aside as a little old man, wrinkled as a walnut, pushed one side open, propped it with a rock as they got twenty feet away, then pushed the other aside and held it. "*Hola,*

hola, amigos," he said with a wave. Then he doffed his hat and stared. He made another effort. "Lorenzo, Paco?"

As they came even with the gate, Ryan handed his reins to Reece and dismounted. The old man waited until Ry was only feet from him, then started to yell. But it was a weak attempt and Ry closed the distance and clamped a hand over the old man's mouth.

He drew his Colt with the other hand, and threatened the old man. "*Señor, habla y* bang bang. *Comprendes?*"

Wide-eyed, the old man nodded. Ryan led him to the rear wagon and helped him up into the bed. "Skeeter, keep him under there with you, and keep him quiet."

As quietly as they could, they clomped on through the village. At the west end was a corral and side-less pole barn full of loose hay, flanked by two eight-foot water troughs. They'd harnessed the best of their mounts, and Ry rode his gray, Reece his sorrel, Ret his steel gray, and McTavish his borrowed dappled gray. Their tack was in the back of the wagons. If they needed to make a fast getaway, they were prepared.

They watered the stock at the troughs, giving them time to drink their fill, and were just reining away when a man called out from the darkness. "*Hey, Joquin, Paco, tiene usted cigarillo?*"

"*No, amigo, no cigarillo,*" Ret called back.

There was a moment of silence, then the man called again, "*Quién es?*"

Ry asked in little more than a whisper, "Can you see him?"

"Nope."

"Let's just move on."

Reece and Ry both gave heels to their mounts and plodded away as Ret and McTavish clucked the teams up and followed.

But the man was not to be ignored. This time from almost directly behind them on the two-track, a louder shout rang out. "*Quién es?*"

They clomped on. He called twice more, before three close shots, as fast as a man could lever in, echoed up and down the canyon and they spurred their mounts and the teams into a gallop.

It was a moment before another tight group of three shots rang up and down between the distant cliffs, now widening to a quarter mile.

Ryan yelled at Reece, "Shooting at us?"

"Nope, signaling the village, I'd guess," he shouted back.

Luckily, the moon had risen and there was a hundred-yard-wide swath of moonlight on the valley floor. Ry and Reece had pulled nearly a hundred yards ahead of the wagons, as, wisely, Ret and McTavish were taking it a little more carefully, giving Ry and Reece time to turn and wave them down if there was trouble.

After a half mile of hard pounding on the two-track, that was exactly what they did, and the drivers pulled their teams to a stop as Ryan reined up beside him.

"What's up?" Ret asked as soon as the wagon settled.

"Dig me out a few sticks of Mr. Nobel's finest, some fuse and a detonator."

"You gonna blast a hole to hide in?" Ret asked.

"Damn creek has cut a ravine twenty feet deep, less than that wide, damn near straight down. Let's blow the bridge. They'll have to follow afoot."

In moments Ret had five sticks and bound them with a length of rein he cut away, sunk the fuse detonator in the center stick and handed it to Ryan, who ran the thirty yards to the timber bridge and disappeared over the side, standing on a lower stringer. He quickly reappeared and waved them forward. As Ret drew even, he yelled at him. "Got a Lucifer?"

Ret had to retreat to the rear of the wagon and his saddlebags, but did so and soon handed a small box over, then again whipped up his team and joined Reece and led McTavish a couple of hundred feet on down the road.

Ryan waited patiently while the others joined up to wait for him. He had only two feet of fuse on the bundle of dynamite, which would only give him two minutes to clear out, but he couldn't get a damn match to light. As he made his third pass with the match, dirt kicked in his face from the roadbed, shots rang out, and he heard the pounding of a dozen oncoming riders.

Two or three more shots buzzed overhead and kicked up gravel, and finally, as his kin began to return fire, did he get flame.

The oncoming riders must have scattered when four rifles opened up on them, giving Ryan time to set the fuse to hissing and spitting sparks.

Then he ran.

"Don't follow too close," he thought to himself, a silent warning to those trying to run them down, as he pounded trail back to his gray that was still being led by Reece. He knew nothing about the people in the village and had no interest in harming innocents. But his task was rescuing Elizabeth, and that came before all else.

They were only another fifty yards when the canyon lit up with a roar that sent shards of cottonwood bridge in every direction, lit up the canyon as if the sky was lined with lightening, and echoed its sharp crack. Then a rolling roar, echoed up and down the canyon, reverberating in the tight confines.

They'd only gone another half mile when two riders bore down on them from the west, but as suspected had no idea a threat was coming from their direction, particularly not in the form of sombrero clad riders and wagons belonging to *Señora* Aracela O'Reilly.

Ry and Reece swung wide as if to obligingly let them pass in the center, only rather than allowing it, both swung their rifles knocking the oncoming guards out of the saddle.

They jumped from their mounts, and Reece yelled, "Tie them?"

"No time," Ryan replied. "Disarm them. Strip the tack of their mounts and chuck it in the weeds and run their mounts off. When they get their senses about them, they'll likely hightail it afoot."

They left the Mexicans moaning on the roadside, without mounts, Winchesters or sidearms, and again were pounding trail, looking for the stairway to the eagle's roost.

Then they saw a campfire, and not far from it, the midget who was among those they'd been hunting. Only this little man was paying little attention to them. He was paying close attention to the bound Mexican upon whose chest he was perched, attention to the tall Mexican's bulging eyes as the Mexican, hands bound behind, bucked, and the little man worked to choke the life out of him.

Chapter Thirty-Six

***

Ryan leaped from his gray and ran for the little man, knocking him rolling off the tall Mexican. The man on his back choked and coughed while the little man scrambled to his feet and clawed for his holstered revolver. The pistol he carried only had a two-inch barrel, which was much easier for the short-armed man to handle. He barely cleared the holster, as did Ryan, when a shot roared out from behind Ry and the little man was blown back, head over heels, until he stacked up, unmoving in a little thicket of greasewood.

Ry glanced back to see Reece's smoking revolver in hand.

Reece shrugged, "Colonel Colt said he made us all the same size. He had blood in his eye and seemed a little upset you didn't let him pop that old boy's eyes out."

Ryan closed the ten feet to where the little man lay tangled in the greasewood, bent, and examined the pistol. Then he broke the revolver open, a brand-new Smith and Wesson .44 Russian with a sawed-off barrel, and walked back to where Reece was still mounted.

"Guess I was pretty damn safe. His pea shooter didn't have any peas."

"Guess he should have remembered that," Reece said.

The tall man was sitting up, hands still bound at his back, still coughing.

Ryan walked over and bent near him. "You gonna live, *amigo*?"

"*Sí*," Don Mateo managed, then coughed again.

"Your name?"

"Don Mateo…" and he coughed again, "Don Mateo Jose Santiago."

"I figured as much." Ryan slipped a folding knife out of his pocket and sawed away on the Don's wrist bindings, then handed him the knife to take care of his ankles.

But the Don didn't try right away, he just sat and rubbed his wrists, his hands coming away bloody. He wiped them on his trousers, and only then sawed away at his ankles. Then he stood, and gave Ry and Reece a short bow.

"I am indebted, *amigo*. But to whom?"

"Ryan O'Rourke and Reece Conner, kin of Miss Elizabeth. Where is she?"

Don Mateo pointed at the carved stairway forty paces to the south. "I would love to go after the Welsh son of a she-dog, but I am shot through the leg."

"There's work down here. How many guards?"

"Only one and the *bandito*, Louie, accompanied the *señorita* up, and the guard returned and moved back to the west. I do not know what lies at the top of the stairway. He talked of a *Señora* Aracela."

As they stood gazing up into the darkness, the two wagons reined up.

"What was the gunfire?" Ret asked.

"That little fella," Ryan said, pointing, "drew on me. Hell of it was, he forgot to load his revolver."

"So, you won a gunfight with a tiny man with an unloaded gun?" Ret said, with a sardonic grin.

"Actually, Reece did."

McTavish walked up with Skeeter close behind. "Not bad shootin'," McTavish said. "Little target like that."

"All of you can clamp your jaws," Reece grumbled. "He forgot to mention his shooter wasn't loaded or I'd been a little easier on the little fella."

"I'm not complaining," Ryan said, but he too was smiling.

"Well, no matter," Reece added, "I'll be judged at St. Peter's gates...right now there's business at hand. There's a village full of angry miners or whatever the hell they are, and they're likely finding a way around that blowed-up bridge—"

"Blown bridge," Ret corrected.

"One of these days..." Reece said, staring at his brother, then he continued. "Let's get the hell up there and see if Miss Elizabeth has any interest in being rescued. Hopefully all them up above are sawing logs."

Ryan glared at Reece. "Of course she wants...." Ry clamped his jaw, then continued. "Remind me to make your ears ring, cousin, when all this is over." Then he shrugged. "I doubt if anyone within five miles is asleep. Sounded like Gettysburg down here. Nobody slept through that."

"No matter," Ret said, still looking up. "She ain't down here, so let's climb Jacob's ladder."

Skeeter questioned that. "Pretty sure the Good Book say Jacob's ladder goes to He'ben, and I'm pretty dang sure that ladder might go to Hell even if'n it is the up direction."

"How much fuse we got?" Ry asked.

"Whole spool full, big spool, could be a thousand feet, maybe more, I'd be guessin'," Skeeter said.

"Sticks?"

"Whole case, less five, and plenty 'dem detonators."

"Skeeter, can you handle the stuff?"

"Yes, sir. Used it to blow big ol' oak stumps outta the fields. Dey called me 'powder man' back on the plantation."

Ry chuckled. "Surprised you didn't slip a stick or two under the owner's four poster bed."

"His missus was kind to the little ones or I mighta gived it a go."

Ry laughed again. "Okay, then I want you to stay down here," Ry requested. "We'll go up, and you rig a couple of sticks each twenty or thirty paces apart, in a fan, say a hundred paces back the way we came...the way those chasing us are coming. Keep placing bombs until you hear them coming or until you run out of fuse."

"I should be going after Miss Elizabeth."

"Doesn't matter if we fetch her safe if we can't get away safe."

"Yes, sir," Skeeter agreed, and turned to go to work.

Ry moved his gaze to Don Mateo. "Can you walk at all?"

"I can limp. Slow, but limp."

"Unharness the stock, get lead ropes on them, and you and McTavish move them away. Carry at least all the bridles. McTavish, we can't get away if we got no mounts, so it's up to you to keep them near. If Skeeter finishes, have him move the saddles too. Then," and he yelled at Skeeter, "When you're done, turn those wagons over," then he remembered the old man was still in the back of one, "for cover and load all the spare weapons. Send the old man back the way we came and don't let him see you spreading surprises all over. Tell him to move his best or you'll shoot him in his skinny ass. With the bombs and three or so Winchesters each, you and the Don here should be able to hold off a small army."

"*Via con Dios*," the Don said. "Kill the Welshman, should he show his ugly *cabeza*."

"I'm sure as hell tired of chasin' him. So, if I get the shot, he's a dead Welshman."

Ryan, Garret and Reece headed for the stairway and began the long climb up.

Chapter Thirty-Seven

* * *

After they'd enjoyed a dozen old Irish folk songs,
and Louie had refused to rejoin them, Elizabeth knew Louie
was deep in his cups. For the first time since she'd known
him, he'd been badly slurring his words. After Aracela had
put away her instrument and complimented Elizabeth on
her voice, she yelled down to where Louie was still perched
on a rock. He didn't bother turning, only remained looking
out over a moonlit Sonoran desert.

Aracela had yelled even louder, "Mr. Bowen, Miss
Graystone and I are retiring. She has instructions to do as
I will do, and that is to shoot anyone who tries her door.
Brigands wandering the hallways will be shot."

"Whores," he shouted, waving over his shoulder, not
even bothering to look around. "That's…that's what…
what all you bloody women…and your ma's and your split
tail whelps be…all be whores."

"I believe," Elizabeth said, "that Mr. Bowen is drunker
than the rat that fell in the vat."

Aracela gave her a tight smile, then shrugged, "He
would be worthless, wallowing in the bed like a boar hog

in a bog. He will be apologetic in the morning." She picked up the two tumblers they'd been sipping her best whiskey from, and she noticed both had a swallow left. She handed Elizabeth's to her, and toasted, "May you be in heaven an hour before the Devil knows you're dead."

And Elizabeth toasted her back, "May you live as long as you want, and never want as long as you live."

They downed the last sip, and each headed for their room.

In the soft bed she fell into a deep, motionless, whiskey-induced slumber.

At first, she thought Louie was banging on her door, and she sat bolt upright. Then she thought it thunder…a Sonoran monsoon. She sat and stared at the window for a moment, waiting for lightning to announce another clap of thunder. But none followed. She arose, threw back the down cover protecting her from the desert night chill, and padded to the single window in the two-story bedroom. No rain. Dry lightning maybe?

She was nearly back asleep when she heard the distant echo of what could only be a gunshot. One quick crack, the sound of which echoed up and down the canyon, which was nearly four hundred yards across the flat below where the stairway terminated.

Something was happening, and it wasn't a thunderstorm.

She heard a door shut. Aracela? Then, she padded to her own and opened it to find Aracela about to knock.

"What?" Elizabeth asked.

"Indians, I imagine," Aracela replied.

"Do they attack at night?" Elizabeth asked.

"Never before, but attacking in the daylight has never worked out for them. The desert Indian is many things, but stupid is not one of them. He seldom makes the same mistake twice. I put nothing past him as a silent and stealthy fighter…even attacking at night should he think it to his advantage. That said, Mr. Bowen and you could have brought trouble to my door. The law has ofttimes been curious about Castile Aguila. My husband was not much of one for company, particularly the law. So, did you lead them here?"

"Not on purpose, Aracela. And please remember, I did not come of my own volition. Had it been my way, I'd be on an elevated stage in Tucson at their opera hall, or in a fine hotel room there."

She seemed to consider that a moment, then changed the subject. "I must make sure my men have arisen?"

"Men?"

Aracela smiled. "No, not the cook nor gardener. The entrance to my distillery cave is only a hundred paces south along the face that rises from our flat. Four of the single men who work for me…work in the distillery but primarily guard for me, former *soldados* from Mexico…live just inside the cavern. I'll return shortly. There's a thick wooden bar under the bed. Bar the door. Twice savages have overrun the castle and I'd hate to see you disappearing on the rump of a Yaqui pony."

With the roar of the dynamite, Louie jerked awake from his recline against the rock he'd been perched upon. He struggled to his feet. Forgetting where he was he nearly walked off the edge of the precipice. He stumbled back, tripping to plop on his butt, shook his head, hard, and slapped himself, and finally was able to focus and rise. He was chilled to the bone, but the castle was nearby. If he knew Aracela and her household, there would be a fire still burning in the great room and he could roll up in the bear rug near the hearth. That is if her personal chamber door was locked and he could not use her silky skin rather than the bear's fur to provide warmth. He sort of remembered being a little insulting to the women, and Aracela had never been one to take an insult lightly. Of course, there was always the songbird. Maybe it was time to pluck her tail feathers. He smiled to himself. Maybe it was time. If he had to sell her, she would, however, be worth far more as a maiden who bloodied the sheets her first time. It had been the only thing to hold him back. But the itch was overtaking his restraint.

He'd just swung aside the massive timber front door, when he heard the familiar crack of a Colt being fired. One time. He would have wondered from which direction it came, were it not for the echo, the reverberating song of the shot's crack bouncing from wall to canyon wall. He had to think...where the hell was his sidearm? Then he remembered. Aracela had insisted he remove it, and belt, holster and revolver hung on a hat rack in the dining room.

Still a little unsteady on his feet, he stumbled through the great room and retrieved his weapon. He strapped it on, wishing he had his Winchester. But it was with his tack and the chestnut Morgan left with the guard down on the flat.

Down where the shot had originated from.

Did Enano find a shell and send his many thousands of dollars of *haciendado* flesh and bone to meet its maker? He hoped not. If so, he'd have to take a quirt to the little man. Or did the Yaqui or Apache slip up and send Enano to hell? Only one way to find out, and that was to descend the stairs and discover for himself.

He knew of Aracela's guards, but put little trust in any band of former Mexican *soldados*. He'd fought with them—

alongside the regulars—and fought against them. Never had he been impressed with them. They were as likely to shoot each other as the enemy and most every Yaqui or Apache coup stick was adorned with a half dozen *soldado* scalps. He'd rather fight alone and as *borracho* as he was than fight with her guards at his back.

He moved back outside and quietly across the landscaped entry and down the trail to the head of the stairway. From the landing on the castle flat, the stairs curved away, turning inside, and only fifty feet below disappeared from sight.

A pair of waist-high boulders flanked the landing, so he chose the one over which he could see the most of the stairway, and hunkered down to wait.

Unfortunately, the stairway was in the moon shadow of the cliffside, and even if the moon was not about to set. He may have the high ground, but the darkness was not his friend.

In the renewed silence, he heard the shuffling of footsteps coming up the carved stairs.

Chapter Thirty-Eight

***

Aracela reached the entrance to her distillery cave, and as was the norm it was twenty degrees warmer than the cool desert air outside. It was the men's custom to leave the door open, thick planks that matched the entry doors to the castle. She wasn't surprised to see Enrico, her *jefe* guard stumbling out in his nightshirt, rubbing his eyes.

"*Señora*, pardon my sleep attire."

"Wake the others, arm yourselves. Let no one top the stairway. No one."

"Yaqui?" he asked, his eyes widening.

"No, Yaqui do not have explosives. Nor do Apache. Be careful as it could be *paisanos* fleeing attackers, but if they do not wear the sombrero…. And the villagers have been warned not to climb the stairway without the signal." Two shots, a pause, and a third shot, was the signal that friendlies were approaching.

"*Sí, señora.* No one reaches the top." He nodded. The cave itself reached so deep into the mountain—a maze of caverns—it had never been fully explored, but at an opening in the canyon wall, a vent had been expanded, landings built top and bottom, and served to hoist barrels and grain and lower finished casks of whiskey. A clever man could climb or even be hoisted to the opening, and attack them from the rear. So, it must be guarded.

The *soldado* guards all carried the 1870 Springfield trap-door .45/70, single-shot rifle, as did the Mexican army from which they'd deserted. It had the advantage of a bayonet, but the disadvantage, as Custer had just learned, of having its copper jacketed bullets stick in the chamber. These then had to be removed with a knife, slowing the gun's rate of fire from seven or eight a minute to one.

"I must return and care for my guests. Remember, Enrico, no one reaches Castile Aguila."

"*Sí, señora,* no one."

★★★

As the kin climbed, Skeeter busily strung fuse from the wagons to the killing field, pacing a hundred strides, placing two sticks deep in the nearest pile of rocks with a detonator, then moving twenty to twenty-five paces laterally, placing another two sticks and a detonator and returning, stringing that fuse back to the wagons. He soon had seven shocking surprises for anyone following.

He'd left Don Mateo and McTavish leading stock away. Then Don Mateo returned and loaded the Winchesters, leaving one or two at each end of the wagons, which were soon to be overturned.

Just as they decided they were as ready as they could be, they heard the approach of hoofbeats and the clank of weapons or harnesses.

"Time to discourage the villagers?" Don Mateo asked. He had fished two cigarillos out of Enano's vest pocket, with the admonition, "You owe me, little man."

He drew deeply on one, making the end glow, and handed it to Skeeter. "You are the powder man, no?"

"I am the powder man, y'all bet." And he touched the glowing end of the cigar to two fuses on bombs that flanked the road a hundred paces to the east.

"And it begins," Don Mateo said, as the flame sputtered away, then added, "I believe we should cause them to hesitate and not pass the little welcomes you've placed."

"Agreed," Skeeter said, and both shouldered Winchesters and fired down the center of the approaching road at unseen targets.

They heard shouting and the snorting of horses as they were raked with the vicious rowels of Spanish spurs.

They could make out the sounds of riders escaping the road to both sides, riders now proceeding with great caution.

***

Aracela strode quickly back to the castle, entering the rear, and making her way to the great room. "Louie!" she called out, then getting no answer decided he was likely passed out where his pouting had taken him, overlooking the desert. No matter, she had no time to worry about him.

She hurried upstairs and rapped on Elizabeth's door and called to her. Elizabeth quickly opened and greeted her, again dressed in her blouse, split leather riding skirt, and doeskin boots.

"Would you share a weapon, Aracela?" she asked.

"I am not pleased with Louie Bowen, Elizabeth, but not so displeased I want to see him shot."

"And if I swore not to shoot Louie?"

Aracela gave her a tight smile. "Maybe later. If there

truly is a threat. Right now we go to the cave while my guards keep us safe."

"If they keep us safe, why do we hide?" Elizabeth asked, but knew it was a facetious question.

"Just follow," Aracela commanded. And they headed for the rear stairway.

***

Ryan was in the lead with Reece and Garret close behind. As they got about halfway up the well-worn stairway, two explosions cracked, lighting the canyon walls, then rumbled. As soon as it quieted enough for them to be heard, Ryan turned back.

"I guess those fellas got across the creek."

Reece chuckled, between deep breaths. "Probably a little sorry they did. Let's go."

"Hold it," Ry said, raising a hand. "Hear that?"

Only slightly above, a narrow trail led away from the stairway toward the mouth of the canyon. And the sound of rapid, crunching footsteps came their way.

"Down," Ry said, and they crouched, staying as inconspicuous as possible, pressed against the canyon wall.

A man in a sombrero came into view only fifty feet away, carrying a scope mounted Springfield. A sharpshooter's weapon.

Ryan let him get only twenty-five feet from the stairway and some ten feet above them, and called out. "Halt, *amigo*. Put your weapon down."

Garret started to repeat the command in Spanish, but the man foolishly swung the muzzle up. It would be his last reckless move, as this time Ryan, out front, beat Reece to the shot. The guard reeled back, the rifle flew away and clattered down the steep cliff, disappearing into the darkness. The man grasped at the slippery side but he was unable to find a handhold, and even had he, the blossoming blood on his chest portended his quick demise. He pitched over the edge, and they saw him bounce only once then disappear into the darkness.

"Sorry, *amigo*," Ry muttered, then turned to his kin. "Likely the guard who took the potshots at approaching visitors."

"Likely," Reece said. "Move on, let's end this."

***

Approaching the stairway, Enrico and his three *soldado* guards hit the ground with the sound of the explosions in the canyon below. They hunkered together, staring into the distance, unwilling to proceed.

"Did Maximo bring the cannon up?" one of the men asked.

"No," Enrico said with a chastising tone. "Two explosions very close together. No one could reload that quickly."

"Then what?"

"Then what is a good question, *estupido*. You think I am a soothsayer?"

"Should we return to the cave?"

"No, you simpleton. We have a job to do. We guard the stairway."

"Then stay low. Shoot anything that moves without the sombrero."

"*Sí*, no sombrero, we shoot."

"And maybe we shoot even with a sombrero. Better they get the last rites than those of us entrusted to guard the *señora*."

***

Louie was taken aback by the explosions. What
the hell was going on? Indians don't have a cannon or dynamite. Were they being attacked by the Mexican Army, or
hell, by Crook's Army out of Camp Verde or Fort Whipple?
What the hell was happening?

When explosions lit the canyon bottom, he got a fleeting
glance of horsebackers and men on foot, but the glances
flashed so quickly he couldn't make out if uniformed. No
matter, whoever they were, they were not the friend of
bandito Llywelyn "Louie" Bowen.

He had not heard the signal of two quick and one later
shot, so whoever had fired that last shot, from somewhere
on the stairway, was no friend of the castle, so no friend
of his.

Where the hell were the guards? he wondered, *Those*
paid to defend Castile Aguila?

Not that it mattered much. He had the high ground,
a boulder for cover, and anyone on the prod coming up
the carved stairs would be right in his sights no more than
fifty feet away.

Chapter Thirty-Nine

* * *

"We're getting close," Ry said to his cousins, close behind.

"I feel like Jonah," Garret said, "paddling into the whale's mouth."

Ryan chuckled. "Maybe I should let you go first?"

"Bugger you, boyo," Garret replied. "She's your sister."

"I'll tell her you said she was my sister, not your cousin. She might take offense and kick you in the *cojones, señor.*"

"Shut up, we're close," Reece said.

Ryan began to do the creep, keeping his back to the wall, side-stepping, leading with his gun hand. His kin followed close behind.

Rounding a gentle curve, he could see only two dozen strides up the stairs, if you took them two at a time, two large boulders framing what must have been the landing. The flat. Eagle Castle. Castile Aguila.

"What do you think?" Ryan whispered to Garret who was next in line.

"I can hear that old whale chomping his lips," Garret said.

"Very amusing. Are you two ready? Let's top out at a run and each head in a different direction."

"Sounds fine as frog's hair. I heard Custer tried the same tactic."

Ryan ignored him and stepped out to make a dash for the top, then his vision was blinded by the flash and roar of a revolver. He was blown back into Garret, who caught him and dragged him back around the curve.

Reece stepped out, firing at the top of the stairs, not at any particular target, but just above the boulder line. He emptied his revolver, fanning it, then he too backed out of sight of the crest.

Louie took a deep breath when he realized someone was very near on the stairway. And they weren't making a casual approach. The man he could see was coming around the curve below, flattening himself against the wall. He wasn't much of a target, but enough.

Then the damn fool swung out, facing him and taking a long step as if he was going to sprint up the stairs.

Louie was carrying the brand-new Merwin & Hulbert .44 he'd taken off that whelp of a city marshal in Wickenburg, and smiled thinking now was as good a time as any to see if he could knock some hooligan off the stairway for a couple of hundred-foot fly to the hard desert below. He had a secure rest on top of the boulder, and took a bead, holding the weapon with both hands.

It had a smooth trigger, hardly more than a one-pound pull. He was almost surprised when it bucked in his hand, but not a bit surprised when the man below flew away like he'd been given both heels by a seventeen-hand mule. Louie was still a little drunk, and he wondered how pure his aim had been. But he smiled to himself. He could hit a dozen peach tins in a row from fifty feet, so that was a heart shot or he wasn't Llywelyn Bowen.

Then surprise returned as the trail below lit with gunfire, and chips from the boulder peppered his face, making him flatten.

Between his shot and those below, all targets were gone, occluded by gun smoke.

How many were there? As fast as fire returned, he figured there must be a half dozen.

Time to beat a trail. He knew there was another way off this flat, away from Castile Aguila. The hoist.

He rose slightly above the boulder and fired three quick shots. Sparking off the hard surface of the cliff's wall below. Then he ran.

***

Enrico and his three fellows were creeping for-ward. There was gunfire ahead.

They were staring into the darkness where the flash of three gunshots had just given them a quick glance of a man, a man without a sombrero.

"Take a knee," Enrico ordered, and stood to the side showing his courage as his three *soldados* dropped down and shouldered their weapons.

The target must be loco, as he did not run away, but rather ran straight at them. One of the soldiers panicked and fired his single-shot trapdoor, then just as quickly threw the weapon aside and ran. Before Enrico could give the order to fire, the oncoming man snapped off two shots, and one of the *soldado's* tumbled back and Enrico felt his chest fill with fire. He dropped his Springfield and the final guard ran, tripping over his *compadre* and stumbling away.

Louie sprinted past, headed for the cave.

***

Aracela and Elizabeth had slipped into the cave.
The living quarters of the four guards were in a walled-off
indentation to the left of the door. To the right was a small
plank bar with four stools, used for tasting as Aracela's habit
was to invite her longest tenured employees to taste each
batch before it was shipped.

Now the plank bar and stools hosted Elizabeth Anne
Graystone and the mistress of Castile Aguila. They were
sipping, not a Castile Aguila product, but rather a fine
French brandy and snacking on Irish cheddar Aracela had
acquired. Aracela called it her European breakfast.

When the last shots rang out, Aracela dismounted from
the stool. She walked to the doorway and opened the heavy
planks, peeked out, and turned back to Elizabeth.

"I had better lock up and we should retreat deeper into
the cave, just in case things get out of hand."

Elizabeth, too, climbed from the stool. "As you wish. I
am at your mercy."

Aracela turned to place a heavy plank to bar the door,
but it flew aside just as she was about to do so, and knocked
her flying. She landed on her butt with an "Oof."

Louie burst through the door.

He strode over to Elizabeth. "I believe, Songbird, I
must take my leave. And, unfortunately for both of us,
leave you here. You have been far too much trouble to
tolerate. I'm only sorry I didn't pleasure you. I will not
leave you for another, so…"

Louie drew the big .44 and placed the muzzle between
Elizabeth's eyes.

"Louie!" Aracela screamed at him.

"And I think you're next," he said, and laughed as he
pulled the trigger.

A sheepish look crept over his face as the hammer fell on a spent cartridge. Then he snapped his head toward the door as he heard footsteps outside. "God smiles on both of you," he said with a growl, then bolted deeper into the cave, his footsteps fading as he did so.

Garret and Reece Conner burst through the doorway, revolvers in hand, panning the broad opening.

Elizabeth ran to them and hugged each one in turn. Then she stepped back with her hands on her hips. "Where the hell by all that's holy have you been?"

Reece and Garret looked at each other and shrugged.

Reece didn't answer the question, rather he poised one of his own. "Was that Bowen that ran in here, and where the hell is he? He's worth a thousand dollars."

It was Aracela who answered. "There's another way out. The hoist we use to raise supplies and lower kegs."

"Where?"

"You won't find it unless you know this cave, and I won't show you. He offered to kill us both before he ran there, and he's had plenty of time to reload by now."

Garret took Elizabeth by the wrist. "Ryan is shot and needs tending."

"How bad?" Elizabeth asked, her fist to her mouth.

"If he had a heart, it would be through it, but as it is it's a shoulder."

"Where is he?" Aracela asked.

"He and a Mexican are out there, probably comparing scars."

"One of my men?" Aracela asked.

"I'd guess, he ain't with us. He's shot in one shoulder and Ryan the other."

"Isn't with us." Reece corrected his brother, rather than the other way around.

"No time for grammar," Ret said, with a smile.

"My woman Adoncia is an excellent healer," Aracela announced. "Get them inside."

Reece turned to Garret, "I'm going back down to get the Don, Skeeter and McTavish, and see if we can get back up here without getting shot."

"You're likely to have to carry the Mexican. He's leg shot."

Aracela picked up on that and suggested, "We have a hoist and—"

Just about that time four more explosions erupted below in quick succession.

"What the hell are you doing to my people?" Aracela asked.

"We're just trying to stay alive," Reece said. "We got this habit of shooting back if you shoot at us."

"I'll go down with you and put a stop to this."

Garret and Elizabeth followed Reece and Aracela out. While Garret and Elizabeth gathered Ryan and the guard up, Reece and Aracela hurried for the stairs and began descending.

When only a quarter way down, Aracela stopped him. "Louie could have beat us down."

"His problem," Reece said, and motioned for her to continue.

Chapter Forty

***

"That's the last of it?" Don Mateo asked Skeeter.

"We got us plenty of shells left, more'n we could shoot in a week, but we used up all the fuse."

"Looks to me like most of them, maybe all of them, have done the *conejo*...the rabbit, and are hunting for holes. All that rock blowing all over hell and gone was pretty damn discouraging."

"What is that?" Don Mateo asked, pointing at something moving far up on the cliffside, nearly a hundred yards back toward the village.

"Dang if I know?" Skeeter said.

Don Mateo jammed a few more in the Winchester 73 and walked toward the apparition on the cliffside. Then he called back over his shoulder, "It's a man. A man on a rope."

He continued until he was only twenty-five strides from where the man would alight, then realized there was a platform, a large platform ten paces by thirty, with a few empty kegs scattered about.

The man was descending a few feet at a time, sitting in

a cask-hitch, lowering himself hand over hand.

"Hey, *gringo*," Don Mateo called out.

Louie looked down. He was still one hundred feet from the platform.

Don Mateo couldn't be sure who it was, until Louie called to him. "Hey, greaser, how did you get loose?"

"Aw, Louie the *bandito*. *Dios* delivers you to me."

"Not yet, greaser."

Louie clawed at his holstered weapon, which he'd reloaded, and even before Don Mateo could shoulder his Winchester, snapped off a shot but the ropes, now swaying with the motion of his draw, had him swinging enough that his aim was off.

Don Mateo seemed to enjoy taking his time, and as Louie was trying to still his precarious position and get another shot off, fired.

Louie seemed to jerk, then he yelled, "Yer a lousy shot, greaser. A lousy…," but his revolver slipped from his hand, plunged down, and hit with a puff of dust. He sagged, then, almost gracefully, leaned back and was upside down, hanging from the cask-hitch with the rope now tangled around an ankle. The hoist was geared, and at only a few feet a second, descended on its own until Louie landed in a heap on the platform.

Don Mateo limped forward, his borrowed rifle at the ready. He reached Louie and toed him, making sure he was no longer a threat.

Then he shot him in the face.

"Do you think you are handsome now, Welshman?" he said, then spat on the prone body. He limped back to where Skeeter waited.

"No love done lost there?" Skeeter asked.

"Nor hate, he was worth neither."

***

Reece moved quickly to join Don Mateo, McTavish and Skeeter at the overturned wagons and was quickly updated on the situation. No shots had been fired since the last series of explosions.

Aracela, still in her nightclothes and a wrap, joined them, and Reece made the introductions.

"We have met," Don Mateo said, "many years ago in Hermosillo when Mr. O'Reilly was still of this earth. Do you recall, *Señora* O'Reilly?"

"I do. You're a difficult man to forget."

"I pray that's a compliment, *Señora*. You are impossible to forget."

"And Bowen?" Reece asked.

"*Señor* Bowen is just over there," Don Mateo said, pointing.

"So, he's down?" Reece said, "and not on the run or shooting at us?"

"Down," McTavish said, "and out. Seems the Don saw him coming and Bowen made the mistake of shootin' at him."

"Out?" Aracela questioned. "You mean—"

"He won't be shootin' at nobody no more," Skeeter said.

"He was..." Aracela began, then got a catch in her throat and turned away.

"Was what?" Reece asked, then added himself, "He was a cold-hearted killer and left many a body of decent folk in his wake. I hope he's buried shallow so the critters get at him."

Aracela continued to look away, and dabbed at her eyes with the wrap.

"You said you wanted to help end this?" Reece pressed her.

She took a deep breath, and turned back to face them. "Hand me a fully loaded rifle."

McTavish glanced at Reece, who nodded, and he handed her a Winchester. She held the muzzle high and fired two quick shots, then a third.

"One of you accompany me, *por favor.*"

"I'll go," Reece said, and grabbed another Winchester and box of shells. He instructed McTavish and the Don. "Protect the stairs. Nobody goes up until we return and give y'all the all clear." He got a nod from both of them and they retook positions at the wagons.

Aracela strode out on the two-track toward the village, after a hundred yards, she repeated the signal, then after another she did so again. In moments voices rang out from the undergrowth, and following her shouts, men began appearing.

When a dozen had gathered around her, she informed them it had all been a mistake. They were to gather their wounded, after they reported many from the shower of rocks from the dynamite, and return to the village.

They seemed reluctant to do so, but soon followed her orders.

By the sunrise, the kin, Don Mateo, Skeeter, McTavish and Aracela were gathered around a roaring fire in the hearth in Castile Aguila. Ryan was sleeping on the bear rug, covered with a buffalo hide. A through-and-through wound in his left shoulder had missed all but a chunk of scapula, and the wound, front and back, was stitched with catgut, and, God willing and it didn't go green, he'd be fit for the saddle in a week. Don Mateo, who Skeeter had carried up piggyback, reclined nearby, his wounded leg propped on a rolled pillow.

After tending to a dead guard and a wounded one,

Aracela had sent her remaining guards down to take care of the three bodies at the foot of the stairway. Her guard—the sharpshooter that Ryan had dispatched—the little man, Enano, and Louie Bowen.

Garret had suggested, "Bowen's hide is worth a thousand dollars. Let us haul him back and collect and we'll leave it on deposit in the Wickenburg bank for the families of those you lost in the last day. And if you like we can sell Bowen's stock, weapons, and tack to add to the loot. The chestnut alone should bring another hundred. All in all we should raise nearly fifteen hundred."

"It was all so unnecessary," Aracela said, her voice quavering a little.

"Well, ma'am, as you recall you had our kin here, against her will."

"But I—"

"But, the fact is, you lie down with dogs you're gonna get fleas. You protect riffraff you may get caught in the wrath they've brought upon themselves. We wish we'd have been able to ride right in and haul Bowen back to the law and our sister back to singing for folks, but we got shot at, and when the kin gets shot at, any one of them, all come running. I'm truly sorry you and yours were in the way, but not a damn bit sorry we got sister and cousin back, nor that your house guest met his maker."

Aracela sighed deeply. "We head north once a year, at least as far as Wickenburg, often all the way to Prescott. Your gesture for the loved ones of those who died is appreciated. Now, I must go to the village and care for the wounded. Adoncia will see to your every need."

"We'll need to be here a while," Reece said. "And by the way, if they haven't freed themselves, you got some freighters and guards tied up out in the desert. You better have someone fetch them afore the pigs eat 'em."

"Thank you. I'll attend to it." She paused a moment, seeming to pick her words. "You are my guests. The *paisanos* in Arizona and Mexico have a saying, 'It is better to be on time than invited.' I guess, for your sister's, cousin's sake, you were on time."

Don Mateo glanced around at the kin, and added, "There's another saying we *haciendados* are fond of repeating, 'Should the Devil himself come calling, we would not bolt the door.'"

Garret laughed. "Well, those sayings are both admirable, but those of us with the Irish in our veins have a saying too…that goes something like this: where the hell is all that whiskey I've been hearing about?"

Elizabeth spoke up, "Mr. Conner, the sun's barely over the horizon. Don't you think it a bit early?"

Ryan opened one eye, and growled, "Early, hell, sister, it's June. That's not too early for the kin to celebrate being together. Fact is, it's way past smooth whiskey sippin' time. And if memory serves, weren't you girding your courage in that cave?"

"Touché," Elizabeth said, and laughed.

Chapter Forty-One

***

While Ryan and Don Mateo healed, enjoying the desert sun and Aracela's huge fireplace in the long evenings, Elizabeth and Aracela visited the village each day and nursed those injured. Garret, Reece and Skeeter helped out rebuilding the bridge they'd destroyed, and enjoyed Aracela's fine, plentiful whiskey and superlative cooking in the evenings. McTavish, with his new mount and tack and two hundred in gold in his poke, returned alone to Wickenburg, against the advice of the kin, which he laughed off as he spent more time alone in the desert than in town. And he missed his donkey, Matilda.

Aracela seemed taken with Don Mateo, and the attraction seemed mutual. She sent four of her men with a wagon load of whiskey, tequila, and pulque, eight kegs, to Hermosillo, with a stop at Don Mateo's rancho with his orders to send ten men and a buggy to escort him home. After delivering Don Mateo's message, Aracela's men were to go on and sell their load.

At the end of a week's time, Ryan, just well enough to ride and hoping a run from savages was not in the offing, set out with Garrett, Reece, Skeeter, and Elizabeth for Tucson. The bridge was rebuilt, and Aracela's men on the mend. Rather than risk Wickenburg or Prescott, they decided to pay the thousand-dollar reward and five hundred for Louie's chestnut Morgan, Enano and Mangas Zaragoza's horses, the two packhorses and the mule and all their tack. They'd try and recover the sum in Tucson. The reward should be easy as the Arizona Territorial Express Company had a major station and offices there. And horses and mules were in demand nearly everywhere in the west.

Elizabeth was thrilled to receive a wire from Sheriff Hatch Stinman informing her they had collected her luggage and all her personal items, and they'd be on the next stage to Tucson, should she so request. She wasted no time returning the communication.

After another week healing and a night enjoying Elizabeth's opening at Tucson's Le Pelletier Opera House, Ryan, Reece and Garret took their leave, riding north.

While settling into her short stay in Tucson, Elizabeth found she had a wire from her agent, Horace Witherham, and discovered she had bookings in San Francisco, Sacramento, Monterey, Santa Barbara, Los Angeles and San Diego over the winter months. She was pleased, and would soon decide if she and Skeeter would take the stage to Yuma or north to ride west in style on the railroad.

The cousins were surprised when they camped outside of Flagstaff and slipped into the Whipple Saloon for a few mugs and a beef steak, and Ryan announced, "I believe I'm turning west here to see if Mr. Beale's road is worth seeing."

"It's a far piece to California," Reece mentioned.

"Hell, it's a far piece to damn near anywhere," Ry laughed. "And I'd like to see that big ol' Pacific Ocean... and I'll bet by the time I reach Kingman I won't have to look at my ugly puss pasted on every damn Ponderosa or roadside rock. Any takers?"

Reece shrugged. "I heard they were paying ten dollars a day for good gun-hands in Leadville. Believe I'll head on that way."

"I'd like to stick with you, cousin," Garret said, "but I ran into a fella in Denver who invited me to study the law with him. I believe I'll wander on up there and talk more with him. Seemed an honest sort."

"You're too damned honest," Ryan said, with a laugh, "to become a lawyer. Hell, next thing you'll want to run for senator or governor and become a real shyster."

Garret gave them a wide grin. "And you two had better be ready to pitch in a bucket full of campaign coin. Remember, a governor can commute your sentence."

"There is that," Ryan said, upended the decent rye the Whipple served, and waved the barmaid over for another round, then toasted, "Here's to kin, and getting Kathleen back whole."

They drank, ordered another and this time toasted to each going their own way…again.

Until the next time the kin called.

A Look at: Nemesis
(The Nemesis Series 1)

The fools killed his family...then made him a
lawman. This wild and wooly western, in the Louis L'amore
tradition, comes from renowned author L. J. Martin, whose
over 20 novels have brought compelling reading to so
many. McBain, broken and beaten from the Civil war, is
reluctant to return to his family, as a snake dwells in his
belly and he can't get the images out of his mind...until he
learns his sister and her family have been murdered. Then
it's retribution time.

AVAILABLE NOW

About the Author

L. J. Martin is the author of over three dozen works of both fiction and non-fiction from Bantam, Avon, Pinnacle and his own Wolfpack Publishing. He lives in, and loves, Montana with his wife, NYT bestselling romantic suspense author Kat Martin. He's been a horse wrangler, cook as both avocation and vocation, volunteer firefighter, real estate broker, general contractor, appraiser, disaster evaluator for FEMA, and traveled a good part of the world, some in his own ketch. A hunter, fisherman, photographer, cook, father and grandfather, he's been car and plane wrecked, visited a number of jusgados and a road camp, and survived cancer twice. He carries a bail-enforcement, bounty hunter, shield. He knows about what he writes about, and tries to write about what he knows.

Also by L. J. Martin

Shadow of the Mast
Rush to Destiny
Unchained
Tin Angel
Blood Mountain
Windfall
West of the War
Bloodlines

Repairman Series
The Repairman
The Bakken
G5, Gee Whiz
Who's On Top
Target Shy & Sexy
Judge, Jury, Desert Fury
No Good Deed
Overflow
The K Factor

The Manhunter Series
Crimson Hit
Bullet Blues
Quiet Ops

The Clint Ryan Series
El Lazo
Against the 7th Flag
The Devil's Bounty
The Benicia Belle
Shadow of the Grizzly
Condor Canyon

The Montana Series – The Clan
McCreed's Law
Stranahan
McKeag's Mountain
Wolf Mountain
O'Rourke's Revenge
Eye For Eye
Revenge Of The Damned

The Nemesis Series
Nemesis
Shadows of Nemesis
Mr. Pettigrew

The Ned Cody Series
Buckshot
Mojave Showdown

CPSIA information can be obtained
at www.ICGtesting.com
Printed in the USA
LVHW042145250421
685564LV00016B/1333